Hard Brakes
Book Two – DI Brakes Investigates
by
Stephen Cohen

Fictional work based on actual WWII events.

Badman publishing

Hard Brakes
ISBN **9798897785759**

Authentic Facts

World War II, Norwich, like so many other towns and cities throughout England experienced significant air raid casualties such as the Baedeker raids, so called due to the apparent fact that Hitler used the renowned travel guide author **Karl Ludwig Johannes Baedeker book** to decide which cities in England to bomb. In April 1942 the raid resulted in the highest number of deaths and injuries in the city, and the city had the highest air raid casualties in Eastern England.

The details are as follows:

- **Baedeker Raids:**

  April 27/28th 1942, German planes bombed Norwich in what became known as the Baedeker raids, targeting historical buildings as identified in the Baedeker guide.

- **Casualties:**

  These raids resulted in the deaths of 229 people and injuries to over 1000 others.

- **Damage:**

  More than 2,000 homes were destroyed, and another 27,000 suffered some damage, with large parts of the city centre in ruins.

- **Other Bombings:**

  Throughout the war, Norwich experienced further bombing, including attacks on factories like Boulton and Paul, and other targets.

- **High Casualties:**

  Norwich had the highest air raid casualties in Eastern England.

- **Other Locations:**

  Great Yarmouth, Cromer, and Sheringham also faced bombing raids during the war.

- **Norfolk Record Office:**
  The Norfolk Record Office holds a "bomb map" detailing more than 600 bombs that fell on Norwich between 1940 and 1945.

The large balloons that flew over London during WWII, designed to deter low-flying enemy aircraft, were called barrage balloons.

Here's a more detailed explanation:

- **Purpose:**

  Barrage balloons were used as a defensive measure to make it difficult for enemy bombers to fly low and attack targets.

- **Design:**

  They were large, uncrewed, tethered balloons that raised steel cables into the air, posing a significant risk to aircraft that flew into them.

- **Impact:**

  The balloons were an iconic feature of the British skyline during the war and were manned by the Women's Auxiliary Air Force.

- **Squadrons:**

  The balloons were grouped into Squadrons like fighter aircrafts.

- **Deployment:**
The barrage balloons were deployed by the American 320th Barrage Balloon Battalion.

- **D-Day:**
The 320th Barrage Balloon Battalion was deployed to ensure that balloons were raised over the landing beaches, especially at night.

CHAPTER ONE

The year was 1942. England's rolling countryside, once a picturesque symbol of tranquillity, had become a landscape marred by war. Bomb craters pockmarked the earth, homes stood in ruin, and the nightly wail of air raid sirens was a constant reminder that death could come from the skies at any moment. Yet, amidst the terror brought by German bombers, there was another shadow creeping across the land, one more insidious and perplexing than any enemy aircraft.

It was a darkness that Detective Inspector Brakes had spent three long years chasing in-between other cases—five bodies, five deaths, each one more inexplicable than the last. His case load, although varied at this time, had nothing to offer him. Each case felt dull and boring, part of the everyday grind and crime that was now war-torn Britain.

And after the lacklustre end to his previous case some months ago, Brakes was simply itching for something to reignite his passion for the chase, and he was certain this case could do exactly that. So, for the first time in months, he unboxed his nemesis.

Brakes sat at his kitchen table in his modest cottage home, staring at the wall in front of him. Plastered across the cracked, faded wallpaper were newspaper clippings, police reports, and photographs, all detailing the five victims who had been found in various locations across the English countryside over the past three years. Each time, the bodies were discovered dressed in different military uniforms, parachutes attached but never deployed. There was something grotesque about the pattern, something that gnawed at the edges of Brakes' mind, refusing to let him rest.

"Five victims, five parachutes. The only links: parachutes, not deployed. Military dress," he muttered, rubbing his chin as he scanned the clippings for the hundredth time. His words bounced off the silent walls, offering no reply.

His home reflected the mind of a man consumed by his work. Every available surface was cluttered with papers, books, and remnants of his investigation. In the corner of the room lay his trusty, half re-assembled Triumph Speed Twin 5T, his beloved 500cc motorbike that Brakes had been restoring after his accident last year.

Initially, it was housed in tangled pieces in the garage, but recently Brakes had needed an easier direct approach, so he moved it into his living room. It had been his one retreat from the madness of war and crime—a place where his hands could focus on something tangible, something that made sense. But the Triumph had gone untouched for weeks now, unloved and gathering dust while the metal lay bare, as his mind remained locked in a different kind of conundrum.

The victims of the cold case had been scattered across the country, their bodies discovered in the most unlikely of places—open farmland, dense forests, rivers, even on top of abandoned bomb shelters. What troubled Brakes most was that, apart from one—an RAF aircraft mechanic—none of the victims had any apparent connection to the military or aviation. Yet there they were found, dressed in military attire, with parachutes strapped to their backs, as if they were part of some sort of military covert exercise that went tragically wrong.

Well, if that was in fact the case, then the mission was doomed from the start. In all five files, not one pilot had given a statement, nor had they been found.

The case had baffled local police, and with the nation's attention on the war effort, these deaths were quickly written off as accidents or errors in parachute deployment. In each case, the medical examiners had concluded that the victims had died from injuries consistent with a high-velocity fall. Their parachutes had failed to open, with the fall killing them on impact.

Brakes winced at that thought. Falling through the sky, desperately pulling at the static line in a final desperate attempt to deploy the chute, only for it to not open. Watching the ground below inching closer and closer, knowing what was about to happen. What goes through someone's mind in this situation? The terrible anticipation of death had to be all-consuming.

Just the mere thought of it sent a chill through Brakes, and his entire body gave a prolonged shudder. Closing his eyes, Brakes forced himself to go through the motion as if he had been there, too.

"Had it been night or daytime? They must have been alone. Apart from the pilot, that is, otherwise surely, someone would have come forward. Then, they jump out of the aircraft. But wait—why weren't they using a static line parachute? Immediately, they reach behind them to open the chute."

"It does not open."

"They try again, blood rushing through their veins like volcanic lava as their heart starts beating faster and faster. They're plummeting through the air at over one hundred miles per hour, and sheer panic finally sets in."

"They start to sweat, grasping at the static line and pulling, pulling, pulling, to no avail. Sweat begins to pour from their body, so much so that not even the fast-flowing air can dry their skin or clothes. Tears begin to sting their eyes, and realisation hits:"

"They are heading to their doom."

"Immediately, they squeeze their eyes shut and hold their breath as they await the inevitable..."

Brakes opened his eyes and immediately headed for the kitchen sink. Splashing some water over his sweat-laden face, he grabbed a flannel and soaked it under the tap. He headed off to his room to change his shirt, making sure to wipe himself down before putting on a fresh one.

What were their final thoughts, Brakes wondered? Was it the fear of what would become of them once they hit the ground, or their loved ones who awaited their return? Sitting down on his bed, Brakes placed his head in his hands and groaned softly.

"Don't do that again, you idiot," he mumbled to himself, moments before a fresh chill ripped through his body.

Heading back downstairs, he buttoned up his shirt whilst casting his eyes back over the evidence in front of him.

Brakes wasn't convinced these cases were separate incidents. Something didn't sit right with him. Why would ordinary civilians—people who had no business being near aircraft or airfields—be found dead in such a manner?

Brakes sighed, falling back in his chair and rubbing his tired eyes. He had been working on these cases unofficially at home for three years now, gathering whatever scraps of information he could in his spare time. His superiors had little patience for his theories, dismissing the deaths as nothing more than tragic accidents. But Brakes' gut told him otherwise. He had been in this line of work long enough to know when something was wrong, and this case had a stench to it, like that of a rotting vegetable lost behind a kitchen cupboard.

His eyes wandered to the old clock on the mantelpiece, its third hand ticking away steadily toward sunrise. He hadn't slept much, his mind too restless to allow for such a luxury. As the first rays of daylight crept through the narrow window above the sink, Brakes stood up and stretched. The cold remnants of last night's tea sat in his cup, but he downed it anyway, savouring the bitter taste.

"Time to see the Chief," he muttered to himself. Heading into the bathroom, Brakes cleaned himself up and readied himself for the day ahead. Pulling his coat from the hook by the door, Brakes slipped it over his dark blue suit, grabbed his hat and opened the door to the early morning chorus of bird song and engines roaring in the distance.

Brakes' timing was perfect; Vera was just pulling up to his house, ready for another day at the station.

Though Brakes' injuries had fully healed from his accident several months prior, the medical officer had yet to sign him off as fit to drive, which meant that he still relied on Vera to drive him around due to his lack of progress on the Triumph.

This had not been the case for the past few weeks, however, as Vera had been on a training programme to officially join the team. Instead, Brakes had to tolerate one of the most introverted constables from the station as his stand in driver. The lad was a stark contrast from Vera and, at one point, Brakes would have relished in his presence. But truth be told, over the past few weeks, Brakes had found he now missed Vera's intense desire for interference.

"Morning, Vera," Brakes said, opening the car door. "Nice to have you back."

"Morning, sir. It's good to be back," Vera grinned, puffing out her chest proudly. "And in my proper uniform, at last."

Brakes couldn't help but smile, pride swelling in his chest. "Welcome to the force, Vera," he said and slid into the seat beside her. "I always knew you would make a great addition to our team. Congratulations."

"Thank you, sir." Vera beamed, her smile wide. "And now that I am an official constable, I won't keep getting told to wait in the car or to stop asking questions."

As the words left her mouth, Vera shot Brakes a playful, accusatory glance and he felt his cheeks grow warm. Clearing his throat, Brakes slammed the car door shut behind him.

"You still might have to make the tea though, Vera," he grumbled, taking his hat off and placing it on the dashboard. "Do try to remember that it's your first week, though. Take things slow, learn the craft." The last part was said encouragingly, earning Brakes a genuine smile from Vera.

As they made their way through the quiet streets of Norwich, Brakes couldn't help but feel the tension creeping into the air. The war had changed everything. The city was no longer the peaceful place it once was. Instead, it had become a maze of ration lines, bomb shelters, and crumbling buildings. Fear was palpable, and it wasn't just the threat of Luftwaffe bombers that hung over the city like a dark cloud.

There was a sense that the very fabric of society was unravelling. People were desperate—rationing, shortages, and constant uncertainty had taken their toll. And now, with the unexplained deaths, it seemed

that even the ground beneath their feet wasn't as solid
and unsoiled as it used to be.

CHAPTER TWO

Brakes and Vera arrived at the police station, a large, austere grey building that loomed over the street. Its imposing structure had always given Brakes a sense of purpose, a reminder of his duty to uphold the law. But today, it felt different—almost like a relic of a world that no longer made sense. Jumping out of the car, Brakes made his way toward the building while Vera went to park.

Strolling through the door with a determined pace, Brakes nodded curtly to the officers he passed but did not pause for polite conversation. His destination was the Chief Commissioner's office, a man Brakes respected but often clashed with.

The Chief was a practical man, one who was grounded in reality and had little time for cases that weren't directly related to the war effort. And that was where the problem lay for Brakes—the cold case that had continued to haunt him was an unsolvable distraction as far as the Chief was concerned. This meant that Brakes should not have considered picking it up again, not when England was still in the throes of an on-going war.

Passing by his desk, Brakes picked up the closed case files and a few completed ones for the Chief to sign off before continuing his journey. Once he found himself in front of the office door, Brakes knocked loudly and waited until a gruff voice called out from behind the obscured glass.

"Come in."

As he entered the office, Brakes was immediately met with a mountain of paperwork. Behind it sat the Chief Commissioner, his round, weathered face framed by a shock of grey hair. Peering over the rim of his glasses, the Chief watched with a mixture of irritation and curiosity as Brakes walked into the office and closed the door.

"Brakes," he said, leaning back in his chair. The Chief then proceeded to throw his glasses amongst the paper on his desk and rubbed a hand across his face. "What can I do for you? I assume you have come to get me up to speed on your current assigned case."

Brakes strode over to the Chief. "Firstly, Chief, can you sign off on these finished cases so I can get them off my desk," he said, dropping the papers in front of him. His superior promptly signed them and immediately handed them back to Brakes before reaching over to grab his teacup. Leaning back in his chair, the Chief took a sip before returning his attention to Brakes.

"Now, how's the black-market case going?" he asked, taking another sip of his tea.

"Well, sir, I've come to talk about the parachute victims' case, actually." Brakes replied, his tone respectful but firm as he lifted the same cold case file he had procured from his desk.

The Chief sighed heavily and shook his head. "Brakes, we've been over this," he said tiredly while placing his teacup down. "The cases are accidents—tragic, yes, but accidents, nonetheless. Each district Chief has signed them off as closed. The war has made everything chaotic. These things happen. Now, let it go, will you.”

“With all due respect, Chief, I don't think that's the case,” Brakes said, stepping closer to the desk. “These people weren't trained soldiers or pilots, which means they had no reason to be near the aircraft or parachutes. And yet, they were found dressed in different military uniforms, which it seems were neither issued nor worn before, with parachutes they'd never used. There is a pattern here, Chief; it's clear to see when you bring all the cases together as I have done.”

“Maybe their sweethearts took them up for a joy ride and they forgot to strap in?” the Chief countered, his voice heavy with fatigue. “We're in the middle of a war, Brakes. There are bombings, spies, black-market dealings. People are desperate; not everything can be explained neatly.”

Brakes shook his head. “I understand that sir. But these deaths...they are not just women but men, too. To other officers there is no pattern, but that's due to no one else having bothered to gather and collate all the information.” Brakes paused, watching the Chief's face. His expression only seeming to grow darker. “These people weren't random casualties— they were either mission training mishaps, or they were murdered. I don't know what the reason is yet, but I intend to find out.”

“You intend to find out?” the Chief barked, slamming his hand down on the desk.

"I'll do it on my own time if I have to, sir. The victims and their families deserve closure, and they deserve to know what really happened," Brakes protested, his face coloured red with determination.

The Chief studied him for a long moment, his gaze hard. Brakes had always been a tenacious detective, and while that quality had served him well in the past, it often led him down path's others wouldn't follow. The Chief knew that Brakes wasn't going to let this go easily.

A few moments of silence filled the Chief's office.

"Alright," the Chief said at last, his tone softening. "I'll give you two weeks. You can dig into these cases, but I need results, Brakes. If you come up empty, you're dropping it. Is that clear?"

Brakes nodded, a flicker of triumph in his eyes. "Understood, sir."

Stepping back, he was ready to leave the room and begin his investigation when the Chief cleared his throat to indicate that Brakes should stay.

"Before you go, Brakes," the Chief began, his voice clear-cut and direct. "As you know, we are short on detective sergeants, so I'm making Constable Stanshore your official partner. She passed the training with flying colours. Her work on your last case was invaluable, and I am certain she'll be a great asset."

Brakes blinked at the Chief's words. Who on earth was Stanshore, and why did the Chief seem so certain that Brakes had already worked with them, let alone knew a person by that name?

"Thank you, sir, but may I ask—*who* is Constable Stanshore?" Brakes asked, frowning. "For what it's worth, I am happy to continue working with Vera."

The Chief scowled and shook his head. "That *is* Vera," he ground out, the muscle in his neck starting to strain. "For God's sake, Brakes. You spent weeks with her by your side, and you're only just finding out her surname *now*?"

Brakes could feel his face warming at the accusation, however true it might be. The Chief watched him through narrowed eyes, and Brakes gave a nervous cough while dropping his own gaze to his feet.

"She is happy with me addressing her by her Christian name. It simply never occurred to me to ask her for her full name," he muttered guiltily, lifting his gaze again to look the Chief in the eye. "And I agree, Chief; Vera will be a great asset to the case, and I am sure that she will be pleased to hear she is continuing to work with me."

"If nothing else, she will at least keep you off that damn motorbike of yours. I and the entirety of Norwich will sleep better if you're kept from controlling moving vehicles of any form," the Chief growled, and Brakes stiffened at his words. Trying his best to school his features, Brakes did his best to show as little emotion as possible while the Chief watched him carefully before finally saying, "That will be all, Brakes."

With a dismissive wave of his hand and a curt nod from the Chief, Brakes turned on his heel and left the office, his mind already racing with possibilities. He had two weeks—two weeks to uncover the truth behind the parachute victims and prove that there was more to these deaths than mere accidents.

Brakes took his completed files back to his desk and placed them in the case closed pile before asking one of the uniformed officers to take them down to the archives. Grabbing his coat and hat, a battle-stricken fedora that now perched slightly askew on his head, Brakes went to look for Vera, who was talking to another officer while drinking some tea.

"Bring the car around, Vera," he instructed her, not bothering to wait for her response before making his way through the station. Once he was outside, Brakes breathed in the fresh air and waited for Vera, who soon stopped the car in front of him.

"Where to, sir?" she asked as Brakes slid into the passenger seat beside her.

"Home, Vera," he said plainly, though he could not contain the smile that was forming on his lips. "We have a case we can finally get our teeth into, and it's going to test those police instincts of yours to the core." At his words, Vera's eyes lit up with excitement.

As they drove down the streets of Norwich, Brakes felt a renewed sense of purpose. This case was unlike anything he had ever worked on before, and it was as if the war itself had opened a door to something darker, something that lurked in the shadows of the human psyche.

And if he was going to solve it, Brakes knew that he would have to venture into those shadows himself.

CHAPTER THREE

During the journey home, Brakes' thoughts drifted back to the first body that had been discovered three years ago. It had been found in a field outside of Norfolk, an RAF aircraft mechanic named Peter Hall.

Hall had been on leave to visit his family when he disappeared. His body had been discovered three days later, dressed in full military gear with a parachute strapped to his back. The parachute had never deployed, and Hall's body showed the kind of trauma one would expect from a high-altitude fall. The coroner had ruled it an accident—parachute failure. But Brakes had never bought that explanation.

Hall had no reason to be flying around the skies, let alone being found in the middle of a field miles from his home, dressed in gear he hadn't been issued. Brakes had questioned Hall's family, his friends and his colleagues, but none of them could explain why Hall had been found like that, and the case had quickly gone cold. But it was only the beginning, and a case like that should never be closed when it had barely even started.

Over the next three years, four more bodies had appeared, each one more baffling than the last. A nurse from London, a shopkeeper from Yorkshire, a butcher's daughter from Kent, and most recently, a farmhand from Derbyshire. All of them dressed in different types of military uniforms, all with parachutes attached, and none of them with any connection to the armed forces, save for Peter Hall the aircraft mechanic.

Brakes had combed through their lives, looking for any hint of a connection between the victims, but he found nothing. They were from different parts of the country, different backgrounds, and had no known ties to each other. It was as if someone had chosen them at random, got them to dress in military gear and then enticed them to jump out of an aircraft and left them to their fate. Even stranger, there weren't any signs of struggle on any of the bodies. At least, none that Brakes or the coroner could see, but no one in their right mind would willingly jump out of an aeroplane while knowing that the parachute on their back wouldn't work.

So why? How?

That was the question that had plagued Brakes' thoughts since taking on the case three years ago, and it was the same question that stood at the forefront of his mind now as Vera drove him home. Why these people? Why this method? And, most disturbingly, why had the parachutes never been deployed? What was the point of these deaths?

Brakes wasn't one to believe in coincidences, and this case was filled with too many unanswered questions to be dismissed as such. There was something larger at play, something that had yet to reveal itself.

When Vera finally pulled up to his cottage, Brakes stepped out of the car and went to unlock the door to his home and stepped inside. He now had two weeks to unravel this mystery and prove to the Chief that these deaths were no accident. Two weeks that would see him revisiting old files and searching for any clues he might have missed. This time, however, he had Vera.

A fresh set of eyes was needed for a case like this, and ones as sharp as Vera's would be a great asset to Brakes. She saw things that even he had missed in their previous case, which meant that by having her officially work alongside him, it was more than likely that Brakes would finally be able to crack this case.

Brakes led Vera into the kitchen where they sat down at his cluttered table, and immediately they started looking through old papers and up at the wall of clippings and photographs. They proceeded to spend the rest of the day and night going over each case, only pausing for quick breaks to replenish their coffee. As the night wore on, splashes of whisky were added for some flavour and much-needed encouragement to keep going.

Before they knew it, another dawn was breaking.

Sitting back in his chair, Brakes stifled a yawn and rubbed a hand over his eyes. "So, Vera, what do you think?" he asked.

"I have to agree with you, sir; the way they all died is the same," Vera replied. Stretching her arms, she blinked back down at one of the cases through tired eyes. "At least, it looks that way."

"How do you mean, 'looks that way?'" asked Brakes, his brow furrowing.

Yawning, Vera pushed back her chair and stretched out her legs before finally replying with a question. "How much do you know about parachutes, sir?"

"Nothing," he admitted, his lips twisting into a frown. "Nothing at all."

Vera sighed. "Neither do I. I am guessing though that there are several ways to tamper with a parachute. If, of course, that is the case with all these." Tapping a finger against her lips, Vera's eyes scanned over the papers again before returning her gaze to Brakes. "It would be prudent to determine that as fact from the start, wouldn't you agree, sir?"

"That's what I concluded, Vera," Brakes said as he ran a hand through his hair. "Thank you for clarifying that. It's good to finally have someone that agrees with me."

Getting up from the table, Brakes and Vera took it in turns to splash water on their faces and freshen up before they headed for the car. They moved as quickly as they could through the city streets on their way to the station and, despite being tired, they were still both functional enough to continue work that day.

That morning was quieter than usual, but Brakes knew better than most that the quiet could be deceptive. The usual peaceful silence that he had equated to rural England was no longer there; rather, it had transformed into an eerie lull that settled between bouts of terror. The hum of warplanes overhead, the sudden drone of bombers in the distance, and the wail of air raid sirens all served as constant reminders that the war was never far away.

Even on this particularly calm morning, as the crisp October air drifted through the streets, the city bore the scars of battle. Buildings stood cracked, streets were littered with rubble from past air raids, and there was an unspoken tension in the air, as if everyone was waiting for the next disaster to strike.

The Norwich police station loomed ahead, a building as tired and battered as the city itself. Inside, the corridors buzzed with the usual activity, officers rushing from one task to another, some looking exhausted from another long night dealing with bombings or curfew violations. But Brakes barely noticed the hustle as he strode through the station, his focus singular and determined. He had something far more pressing on his mind than the day-to-day grind of wartime policing.

Arriving at Chief's office, Brakes knocked twice and entered without waiting for a response. The Chief looked up from behind his cluttered desk, a look of exasperation flashing across his face before he let out a long, familiar sigh as Brakes approached, a thick folder of case files tucked under his arm.

"Brakes," the Chief greeted him, his voice gruff and weary. "What is that file in your hand?"

Brakes laid the folder down on the desk with a deliberate thud. The impact echoed in the small office, as if to punctuate the point he was about to make.

"Everything I have on the parachute case, Chief. Officer reports, photo's, newspaper clipping and family statements." Brakes explained firmly. "There's clearly a pattern in these cases, and I'm not talking about just bad luck or coincidence."

The Chief raised an eyebrow, leaning back in his chair and crossing his arms over his chest. His gaze remained steady, but his expression was one of a man who had heard this all before.

"You've been saying that for years, and I have already given you two weeks to investigate these cases. So, why are you bothering me with this again?" the Chief asked with a heavy sigh.

"Well, Chief, Vera and I have taken another look at the files and Vera agrees with me that it's worthy of further investigation." Brakes said, noting the growing tension in the Chief's jaw. "But it's going to take longer than two weeks. I thought if you took a look yourself, you might come to the same conclusion and grant us an open time scale on this."

The Chief sighed again and looked down at the files Brakes had placed before him. After a moment of silence, he finally leaned forward and picked up the folder to inspect, his discerning eyes roving over it.

"Okay, I will take a quick look over this, Brakes. But to take this further, I need to see hard evidence, or at least something that piques my interest."

Silence permeated the room while the Chief scanned through every piece of paper. Brakes watched as the shook his head or gave the odd grunt, unsure if the indiscernible noises were made in agreement or not.

"I am sure you can see now that I need more time, Chief." Brakes said, pressing the matter. "Two weeks simply isn't long enough to really get into this case."

Brakes expected some resistance. Yes, he had two weeks, but if he could somehow sway the Chief, then he might get more time to focus on the case. The war had everyone spread thin, and cases like this—ones that couldn't be easily explained or connected to the larger threat of invasion or sabotage—were pushed to the bottom of the pile. So, the full backing of the Chief meant he might get less brick walls and hurdles to overcome from other stations and officers.

The Chief's silence as he sifted through the papers was deafening and Brakes was growing impatient.

"Look, I know we're all stretched thin, and I know that these cases don't seem like a priority compared to the black-market thefts or the bombings," Brakes said, his tone growing more urgent now. "But I've been over the reports, every detail. These people—the victims—none of them had any reason to be in military gear, let alone falling out of the sky with parachutes that didn't deploy."

The Chief rubbed his temples again, clearly weary of the conversation, but he didn't interrupt. He respected Brakes enough to let him make his case, even if he had heard it all before.

"The bodies were found scattered across the countryside," Brakes continued. "Different counties, different walks of life—there's no connection between them apart from the way they were found, that is. A farmhand, a nurse, a shopkeeper... they were ordinary people. Except for the first victim, none of them had any links to the military. And yet, they were all found in military gear with parachutes strapped to their backs. That's not a coincidence, sir."

The Chief leaned forward, his eyes narrowing as he considered Brakes' words. Slamming the file shut, he stood up from his chair and threw it back onto the desk.

"You're suggesting this might be a serial killer," he said slowly, more as a statement than a question.

"I'm suggesting that in my view, all these cases are connected, and yes, I think perpetrated by the same person or persons," Brakes replied, his voice low. "These weren't just random accidents. Someone dressed them, staged them—these people were made to look like they were part of something they had no connection to. But I can't tell you why, not yet. Not without more time to dig. Two weeks isn't anywhere near long enough, Chief. You must see that now?"

The Chief let out another long sigh and pinched the bridge of his nose. He had always trusted Brakes' instincts, but this case—this strange, inexplicable series of deaths—was drawing resources away from more local pressing matters. Theft, smuggling, even the threat of espionage was on the rise in Norwich, and Brakes had been assigned to deal with the black-market cases. That was where his attention was supposed to be.

"We've got local problems, Brakes," the Chief said, his tone shifting to something softer. "The black-market thefts are getting worse, and we can't afford to let that go unchecked. The war's stretched everyone to the breaking point, and the last thing we need is people hoarding or smuggling goods. And frankly, you need to put a stop to it."

Brakes' jaw clenched, frustration bubbling beneath the surface. He knew the black-market cases were important, but this—this was something different.

"Vera and I will handle the black-market cases," Brakes said curtly, his brow furrowing as he spoke. "But I need time with these cold cases, too. I think we can agree something is amiss here, Chief. Something sinister."

For what seemed a long moment, the Chief said nothing. He studied Brakes with a tired, resigned expression, as though he were weighing the detective's words against the harsh realities of the situation. Sitting back down, he leaned back in his chair with a groan and gave a slow, reluctant nod.

"Alright," the Chief said at last. "But if you're wrong—if you don't find anything more—you're dropping this, Brakes, and it's your head on the line. Understood?"

Brakes nodded, picking up the file from the Chief's desk and already heading for the door while flipping open the folder. "Understood, Chief." Brakes replied with eager anticipation and exited the room.

Outside the office, the station was still abuzz with work and chattering officers, but Brakes had no time for distractions. He had a list of officers who had worked on the original individual parachute cases, and that was where he intended to start his investigation. But first, he needed to find a parachute expert.

Something had been overlooked—something that would explain the randomness of the victims and, at the very least, if they had all died by the same method. He just had to find the facts.

CHAPTER FOUR

Brakes had always believed that randomness itself could be a kind of pattern. In his years as a detective, he had learned that people who appeared to be chosen at random were often connected in ways that weren't immediately obvious. The challenge was finding those connections, teasing out the threads that linked the seemingly unlinked.

Making his way through the station, Brakes found Vera at another officer's desk, tired but still standing. Clutching the cold case files close, he offered her a curt nod before asking her to bring the car round, and quickly.

Striding over to his own desk, Brakes searched over the side to find what he was looking for. An undeployed parachute, evidence provided from the last body they had found near Kelstern, Lincolnshire. Maybe with this he would find some answers.

Picking it up, Brakes made his way outside, refusing to stop for idle chit chat or pleasantries with his colleagues. He had a mystery to solve, and there was no doubt that there was much work to be done now that he had time on his side.

Vera was already waiting for him at the front of the station. Pulling open the door to the backseat, Brakes threw the parachute onto the backseat before walking to the front of the car.

"We'll be going to RAF Mousehold Heath today, Vera," Brakes instructed the moment he got into the car. "We're going to visit my friend, Doug. He will be able to give us a full explanation on how parachutes work and if this one has been tampered with. If anyone can shine a light on this situation, it will be him."

"Understood, sir," Vera said, pulling out of the station.

The drive to the RAF base wasn't very long, taking only fifteen minutes total with an additional five or so minutes spent at the gate. Despite the guard already knowing who Brakes was, both he and Vera still had to show their identification to be allowed access to the base, as was the proper protocol.

Once they were logged in on the visitor's log, the guard rang for the flight lieutenant to inform him that he had visitors on the premises. Once that was done, he turned back to Brakes and Vera and directed them where to park and instructed them to wait for Flight Lieutenant Douglas Yates.

It didn't take long before there was a knock on the car window. Brakes looked up to see his friend, Doug, his smile wide and familiar as Brakes threw open the car door and jumped out.

"Hey, man. Great to see you!" Doug grinned, taking Brakes' outstretched hand for an enthusiastic shake.

"Doug," Brakes returned the gesture with a wane smile. "Sorry to drop in unannounced, my friend, but we urgently need your help with this case."

Doug's face crinkled, his eyes lighting up with excitement. "You're on a case and need my help, eh? How exciting!" He laughed, finally letting go of Brakes' hand. "But I teach people how to fly, Brakes; I don't know how to conduct an investigation. Whatever would you need from *me?*"

Turning to the rear door of the car, Brakes opened it and pulled out the parachute from the back seat.

"We need you to run us through how one of these works, Doug." he said, watching as Doug's expression turned to one of puzzlement. "And a cup of coffee wouldn't go amiss, either."

At that moment, Vera emerged from the car while placing a cap on her head, completing her uniform. As she rounded the car to stand beside Brakes, Doug looked up and gave his friend a smug grin and a wink.

"Oh, sorry, Doug. This is Constable Stanshore, my partner and driver," Brakes said, nodding over to Vera before shooting his friend a warning look. "None of your monkey business, now. She is here on official police business."

Rolling his eyes, Doug shot Vera a playful smile which she did not return. "Alright, Brakes. I hear you," he chuckled and turned on his heel. "Now, follow me and let's get the kettle on." With a wave of his hand, Doug marched forward.

Following close behind, Brakes and Vera were led through a large hanger and into an office block that took them into Doug's office. As they passed an orderly, Doug quickly pulled them aside to request coffee for everyone before ushering Brakes and Vera into the office and closing the door behind him.

"Okay, let's see what you have here," Doug said, taking the parachute from Brakes to look over it carefully while Brakes and Vera removed their hats and coats.

"Now, Doug; please remember, we know nothing about these," Brakes said slowly, watching as Doug's careful eye roved over the undeployed parachute. "So, use simple language where necessary, if you will."

Doug only nodded in response, his lips curving into a frown as he inspected the parachute. Placing it on his desk, he turned it over before finally speaking up after a long pause of silence.

"This is the British GQ X-Type parachute, and it comprises of four main parts. One, the parachute, two, the inner bag, three, the outer bag and finally, the harness." Doug explained slowly, pointing to each part as he did so. "It's made from silk, cotton and nylon, with twenty-eight rigging lines which attach the harness to the canopy. Decent speed once deployed, going at about ten miles per hour."

As Doug described each part, the orderly arrived with a tray of cups and coffee. Taking it from his hands, Brakes thanked the man before placing the tray on the edge of Doug's desk and started pouring a cup of coffee for each of them.

"So, how does this work?" he asked, handing the first cup to Doug and another to Vera before finally picking up his own.

Taking a generous sip of his coffee, Doug then placed the cup down on the desk as he continued. "See these two vertical pockets on the back? This is where the deployment static line is stowed," he said, pointing at the parachute as Brakes and Vera leaned in, listening with rapt attention. "This line is approximately three and a half metres long; it has this heavy stainless-steel V-ring which is hooked onto a line in the plane prior to a person jumping. It's a great piece of kit once the line is attached; all you need to do is close your eyes, cross your heart and jump."

Brakes nodded, taking a sip of his coffee as Vera stepped forward, her keen eyes scanning over the parachute.

"Okay, so, it's easy to use," she said, turning her attention to Doug. "But why wasn't this one deployed?"

"Simple answer: the static line wasn't attached." Doug's mouth curled into a frown, his brows coming together as he stared at the parachute. "It's only stowed in these pockets to prevent you from tripping over it whilst you're entering the aircraft. Once airborne and nearing your target, a fellow jumper would pull this out and hand it to you, ready for you to hook on. Just like this, look."

Moving around the desk, Doug began pulling the static line from the parachute pockets. A second later, his eyebrows shot up to his hairline and his eyes grew wide.

"Wait a bloody minute... What's going on here?" Peering closer, Doug pulled at the static line with a curious expression. "Someone's tampered with the parachute!"

At his friend's statement, Brakes' heart all but leapt into his throat. "In what way, Doug?" he asked, stepping closer to see what Doug had spotted.

"Here, look." Doug pointed at the pockets, his eyes narrowed. "Someone has sewn the line into the pockets. In fact..." Doug paused and looked at the other pocket, his brow creasing even more at what he found. "Both of them have the lines sewn in. If that hadn't been done, this parachute would have worked properly."

Brakes watched as a flicker of concern crossed Doug's face before looking back down at the pockets. Leaning even closer forward, he and Vera examined the pockets and saw that Doug was right; it was clear that the lines had in fact been sewn in on both sides in both pockets.

"Whoever did this tried to hide the sabotage," Brakes mumbled, his fingers tracing over the stitching carefully. "You can see that they used the existing stitch lines to try and hide their own work."

"We will have to check the others, sir," Vera said as she scanned the stitches herself. "Once we return to the station, that is."

Nodding, Brakes stepped aside and turned back to Doug, who picked up his cup and took another sip of coffee, concern still clear on his face.

"One final question, Doug," Brakes said, meeting his friends gaze. "If you forgot to hook up on the line in the plane, could you still pull on this yourself to open the parachute?"

"In theory, yes, I suppose you could," Doug said, though he did not sound confident in his answer. "But to my knowledge it's never been attempted before. Most people are not that stupid as to forget to hook up. Besides, they have their hand on it all the way to the door. They or the person behind them would notice within seconds."

Taking out his notebook and a pencil, Brakes scribbled down a few notes as before returning them to his pocket. With a quick nod to Vera, he turned back to Doug and gave his friend a polite a nod.

"Thanks, Doug. You have helped us more than you know." he said, clapping a hand to Doug's shoulder. "I owe you a pint or two if you're out later."

This seemed to help Doug's mood, because seconds later he was grinning, his eyes twinkling at the mention of a drink. "I'll catch you in the Bell around seven then, Brakes," he chuckled, finishing off his coffee. "Good luck with the case."

Slinging the parachute over his shoulder, Brakes bade his goodbyes to Doug while Vera collected their coats and hats, and they made their way out of the office and headed toward the car.

Vera drove back to the station a little faster than usual. Clearly, she was eager to check the other parachutes, Brakes thought. Once they arrived, she dropped Brakes off in front of the station as usual and hurriedly went to find a parking spot.

Brakes had barely been at his desk five minutes when Vera appeared before him, her body practically buzzing with excitement while she watched him deposit all the parachutes he had been sent as evidence back when the case first opened. Once he had checked they were all there, Vera pulled up a seat beside him to start checking if the other parachutes had been tampered with in the same way as the one Doug had inspected.

It took them less than five minutes before they found the same issue with all the other parachutes, making this their first piece of concrete evidence that the victims had been murdered. And by the looks of it, it had been someone very cold and calculating.

"Vera, grab a piece of chalk and mark all the parachutes, please." Brakes instructed her. From his periphery, he could see her grabbing a piece from his desk and doing as he asked. "Now, all we need to do is find a link between the victims. There must be something we have missed."

Once Vera had outlined the stitching, they returned their focus to the original files on the five victims.

Peter Hall, the RAF mechanic, had been the first, his body discovered in a field just outside of Norfolk. At the time, Hall's death had been dismissed as an unfortunate accident—a case of parachute failure during a routine training exercise. But Brakes had always been sceptical of that explanation. Hall wasn't a paratrooper—he was a mechanic. There was no reason for him to be jumping out of planes.

Then came Margaret Lane, a nurse from London whose body had been found near a riverbank, her parachute tangled in the branches of a tree. Like Hall, she had no known connection to the military beyond her service as a civilian nurse. Next was George Riley, a shopkeeper from Yorkshire, followed by Jane Wilkes, a butcher's daughter from Kent, and finally, Thomas Gray, a farmhand from Lincolnshire.

Brakes' mind raced as he pored over the reports, searching for something—anything—that might explain why these people had been targeted. He studied their backgrounds, their families, their daily routines. On the surface, they appeared to have nothing in common—no shared history, no overlapping acquaintances. But Brakes knew that appearances could be deceiving.

The unpredictability of the victims felt deliberate, as though someone had gone out of their way to ensure there would be no obvious connections between them. But the more Brakes thought about it, the more he realised that the very lack of connection might be the key to understanding the case. Someone—whoever was behind these deaths—was trying to hide something, to create the illusion of accidents. But why? What were they trying to conceal?

Brakes and Vera spent the next several days tracking down the officers who had worked the original cases, re-interviewing them and reviewing their notes. Many of them had since moved on to other assignments, but a few were still stationed at the same posts. The most helpful of the lot was Sergeant Thomas McLeod, a grizzled veteran of the force who had been one of the first on the scene at Peter Hall's death.

"I remember that case like it was yesterday," McLeod said, his voice rough and gravelly from years of smoking. "We all thought it was strange, finding a body like that. Not every day you see someone fall out of the sky with a parachute that didn't deploy."

Brakes nodded, scribbling notes as McLeod spoke. "Did anything about the scene strike you as odd? Anything that didn't quite fit?" Brakes asked, looking up from his notebook.

McLeod scratched his head, his brow furrowing in thought. "Nothing at all apart from the un-deployed parachute. Let's face it; it's not every day you come across a person attached to a parachute, looking like their whole skeleton had collapsed inside them. It was a gruesome sight and one I will never forget."

"You didn't leave anything out of your report, did you?" Brakes asked. Trying to keep his voice steady, he looked McLeod square in the eye. "Did you have the parachute examined by an expert?"

McLeod shrugged. "I mentioned it in my report, but it didn't go anywhere. The higher-ups weren't interested; said it was a waste of time and effort. They insisted it was just a tragic accident and told me to move on. Too much else going on with the war."

    Brakes clenched his jaw. That was the problem; in a time of war, everything was chaos. But chaos was the perpetrators friend, and maybe that was the point.

CHAPTER FIVE

Brakes paced the floor beside his desk, his steps measured but tense, as if each footfall carried the weight of the unsolved murders that had gnawed at him for years. The walls of Norwich police station buzzed with the sound of officers scurrying between cases, the ceaseless ringing of telephones, and the occasional sharp orders barked by superiors. But for Brakes, all that noise was drowned out by the persistent hum of frustration that had lodged itself deep in his mind.

The walls near his desk were now covered with the newspaper clippings, photographs, and scribbled notes tacked in a chaotic but meaningful pattern from his home. There were articles from *The Times* and the local Norwich and other local papers, reports of bodies found in the countryside, their tragic discoveries barely more than a blip in the chaos of wartime news. There were police files, photographs of victims, close-ups of their faces frozen in death and images of crumpled bulging parachutes beside the still bodies. To the casual observer, it might have looked like a grim collage of unrelated tragedies, but now they had evidence to the contrary.

His eyes moved across the tacked-up headlines, the familiar words now burnt into his memory: *"Man Found Dead Near Wiltshire Airfield... Body of Woman Discovered in Remote Essex Countryside... Parachute Failure: man falls to his death..."* Each one seemingly unconnected despite their similarities, and yet...

Brakes continued to pace around his desk, his mind desperately searching for his next move. It was clear that something more sinister was at play, something deliberate. He could feel it in his gut, but so far, he had only been able to prove that the parachutes had been tampered with. Now he needed to find out if it had been done by the same person or persons.

His pacing stopped, and he stood in front of the wall of clippings, his brow furrowed, arms crossed over his chest. The more he stared at it, the more he tried to piece together what he knew, to form a clearer picture of the pattern he was certain lay beneath the surface of these victims.

Perhaps the parachutes were more than just a tool of death. Could it be that they were part of a message, or even a game that someone was playing? Rubbing his jaw, Brakes stared at the wall for a moment longer before finally tearing his gaze away with a sigh. It was time to bring the Chief up to date. At least now he had some solid evidence to show him.

Clutching one of the parachutes, Brakes headed for the Chief's office. Knocking on the door with a flourish of enthusiasm he didn't usually have, Brakes waited for the Chief to respond.

"Yes," the gravelly voice behind the closed-door shouted. Brakes entered and promptly shut the door behind him.

"Here is your evidence, Chief." Brakes said, all but thrusting the parachute toward his superior, who scowled at the detective's actions. "Take a look at this;

you can clearly see that it has been tampered with and so have the other four. It's murder, no doubt about it."

At Brakes' insistence, the Chief looked down at the parachute that had been forced onto him and sighed.

"I can tell you're excited Brakes, but slow down," he muttered, getting up from his seat and walking around the desk. "Now, let me take a look at what you have here."

Taking the parachute from Brakes, the Chief carefully looked over it with a frown. After a moment of silence, he returned his gaze to Brakes, his eyebrow arching high in question.

"Explain it to me," he said simply, the parachute still firmly in his grasp as Brakes stepped forward to show his findings.

"As you can see here Chief, the line has been sewn in to stop the parachute from being deployed," Brakes murmured, pointing to the pockets as the Chief watched with keen eyes. "Vera and I have confirmed that it's the same for all the parachutes found at the scene of their respective crimes. Though we have no proof of it yet, we believe that it was done by the same hand."

The Chief didn't utter a word as he trailed his fingertips over the pockets, as if memorising the seams that had sabotaged the parachutes. Brakes continued.

"You see, sir, no man or woman would be willing to jump from a plane knowing their parachute would never deploy." he explained, "This was murder, clear as day. Even you can see that now, Chief."

The Chief merely nodded as he handed the parachute back to Brakes, his eyes set with renewed understanding. There was no longer any room to fight Brakes on this, not when he was finally faced with hard evidence that the parachutes had, in fact, been tampered with.

"Your instincts seem to have been correct, Brakes. Good work," the Chief said, a touch of bitterness in his voice. "Now, what do you need from me?"

"It's been years since the last victim, and due to them been spread all over the country, we need an all-stations alert." Brakes explained, throwing the parachute over his shoulder. "And anyone found even remotely like our five other victims is to be reported back to us immediately, sir."

With an agreeing nod, the Chief moved back around his desk and took the phone in his hand.

"I'll send word to Scotland Yard and request that an all-station bulletin be placed," he replied, his tone authoritative. "Now, back to work, Brakes." And without another word, the Chief sat down in his chair and started dialling as Brakes promptly left the office.

Brakes headed back to his desk with a noticeable skip in his step. Throwing the parachute back on the pile in the corner next to his desk, he turned to Vera who was studying the wall and said, "We have an all-station alert going out. We will be informed if any further victims turn up."

"Ah, well done, sir. That's progress for sure." Vera replied, barely taking her eyes off the images and newspaper clippings as Brakes stood beside her, his own gaze turning back to the wall again in contemplation.

Despite the victims' connection, there was still no common thread linking their lives together, and Brakes was not satisfied with that explanation, or lack thereof. Yet the fact the deaths had occurred over such a long period of time, in different parts of the country, only reinforced his belief that he had a possible serial killer on his hands.

His frustration mounted as he turned away from the wall of clippings and moved to his desk. The chair creaked under his weight as he sat down. He had memorised the details of each case and each death told a story, but it was a story with a tragic ending, one without answers. And without answers, the case would continue to dangle in a state of limbo.

Brakes leaned back in his chair, staring at the ceiling as if those very answers might be written there in the cracks of the plaster. He had considered every angle, every possible explanation back when the case first opened. But without any further leads, he couldn't go any further. Exhuming the bodies for a fresh autopsy would require something more than a gut feeling, and despite now having a solid link, he needed more.

What he needed was a new case, a fresh incident that could hopefully give him the clues he was missing. A pattern was emerging, but it wasn't complete yet. If there was another victim, another body with the same strange circumstances, it might reveal something new. Well, that was Brakes' deepest hope. But until that happened, he was stuck in limbo, chasing down stolen goods in Norwich's black-market trade while the parachute deaths remained an unsolved enigma in the back of his mind.

He hated waiting. It was the most unbearable part of the job. The sense of helplessness, the gnawing doubt that maybe he was wrong, that maybe there was no deeper conspiracy and that everyone else was right—these deaths were just tragic accidents after all.

But no. Brakes shook his head. He wasn't wrong. He couldn't be. The pattern was there, which he had now proved. That, and he had the Chief and Vera on his side.

In the meantime, there was work to be done. Norwich was no stranger to crime, and the war had only made things worse. With rations in place and goods in short supply, the black market had flourished. Brakes had been assigned to investigate the increasing number of thefts in the area—smuggled goods, stolen ration books and illegal trading. It was important work, but it felt insignificant compared to the parachute deaths.

The stolen goods and black-market cases were a far cry from the complexity of the murders, but Brakes threw himself into the work regardless.

Over the next six- or seven-months Vera and Brakes had visited warehouses, questioned known smugglers and tracked down leads that usually ended in dead ends or minor arrests. The black-market trade in Norwich was like a hydra—cut off one head, and two more grew in its place. The city's proximity to the coast made it a prime location for smugglers, and with the war going on, everyone was looking to make a quick profit.

Brakes had made several arrests in recent weeks, busting up smaller smuggling rings that had been dealing in stolen cigarettes and luxury goods, but it hadn't been enough to curb the tide of illegal activity. And while he dutifully followed up on each new lead, his mind kept drifting back to the parachute deaths. Vera didn't help the course much either, what with her constant questions.

"If we are dealing with a serial killer, how are they choosing their victims, sir?" she asked, only adding more questions to an already impossible case.

"I don't know, Vera!" Brakes barked, rubbing a hand over his face and sighing loudly. "What I do know is that this case is giving me a headache." Throwing down the file that he had been reading, Brakes leaned his elbows on the desk and shook his head. "I get that due to the sheer distance between the bodies, different counties and all that, things can get overlooked. Add in the fact we are at war, that makes it even more plausible for things to be missed. But are people so blinded by war that they can't or will not see the parachute link?"

Slamming a hand down onto the desk, Brakes found himself at a loss. There had to be connection there, hidden in the layers of detail, and he couldn't shake the feeling that the black-market cases and the deaths might be linked somehow. Or was he just clutching at straws now?

War created strange bedfellows, after all. People with no reason to associate under normal circumstances found themselves entangled in dangerous webs during times of conflict. Could the victims have stumbled upon something they weren't supposed to see? Could their deaths have been staged to cover up a larger crime?

Brakes didn't have the answers yet, but the possibilities nagged at him.

A Conversation with Mayhew

It was late afternoon when Sergeant Mayhew walked into the station. He was a young officer, barely out of his twenties, with sharp eyes and a quick mind. Brakes liked him well enough, though Mayhew tended to follow protocol a little too closely for his taste.

"Got a minute, sir?" Mayhew asked. Without hesitation, Brakes gestured for him to sit, closing the file on his desk.

"What's on your mind, Sergeant?"

"Just thought you'd like to know we've had a tip-off about another black-market deal going down near the docks," Mayhew said, sitting down in the chair across from Brakes. "Could be nothing, but it sounds like there's a shipment coming in tonight. Cigarettes and other contraband."

Brakes nodded, though his mind was elsewhere. "Thank you, Sergeant, we'll follow up on it. Anything else?"

Mayhew hesitated, glancing at the wall of clippings behind Brakes. "You're still working on those parachute cases, aren't you?"

Brakes raised an eyebrow. "What of it?"

"It's just... well, there's talk among the men that maybe you're chasing shadows." Mayhew said carefully. "No offense, sir, but it's been almost a year and there hasn't been any new evidence. Maybe it's time to let it go."

Brakes felt a flash of irritation but kept his voice steady. "I'll let it go when I have answers."

Mayhew nodded, looking unconvinced but unwilling to push further. "Alright, sir. Just thought I'd mention it."

Brakes watched as Mayhew walked away from his desk, his footsteps bouncing off the walls. Chasing shadows. That's what they all thought of him now. At one point, everyone in the station had stood behind him, like a row of dominoes ready to fall the second he did. Now, it seemed as if they were all standing against him.

But Brakes knew better. There was something in those shadows, something that had taken five lives and would likely take more if he didn't uncover the truth.

Even if the waiting game continued, Brakes wasn't about to give up. He just had to be ready for the next break in the case.

CHAPTER SIX

Since taking up the cold case with Brakes, the days had been long and a touch unfulfilling. With each failure to find new evidence or even a small clue to propel the case forward, Vera had watched the detective slowly fall into despair, his obsession with case only seeming to grow.

He hid his despair well, of course; Brakes was not the kind of man to let others see him in a moment of weakness. Yet Vera knew him better than others did, or at least she hoped she did, and watching him lose his love of the chase over the past year was admittedly quite harrowing. More often than not, she wondered what she could do to bring back the spark Brakes had once held for his work.

So far, she had found no answers herself as to how she might help Brakes. So, she simply continued working alongside him, chasing the black-market cases all while doing her best to aid him in his search for answers with the cold case.

On that particular day, Vera was focused on some paperwork that had landed on her desk while Brakes looked through some recent case files. It was a slow work day for them both, one where the clock hands barely seemed to move despite incessantly ticking above their heads.

Then, as if to break them from the stillness that pervaded their desks, Vera caught sight of Seargent Mayhew coming their way, his posture rigid as he stopped before Brakes and requested a word.

Vera truly did not know what to make of Mayhew herself, but she was aware that Brakes considered him sharp for his age. Sifting through her paperwork and making sure to look busy, she leaned a little closer to her desk with the hope of picking up even a snippet of Mayhew's conversation with Brakes.

"... Cigarettes, and other contraband."

Ah. Yet another black-market case. That would keep Brakes occupied for the moment. Huffing out a small sigh, Vera shuffled the papers in her hands before something else Mayhew had said caught her attention.

"No offense, sir, but it's been almost a year, and there hasn't been any new evidence. Maybe it's time to let it go."

Vera stilled in her seat. Where on earth had Mayhew found the courage to talk to Brakes like that, let alone tell him to drop a case that was so clearly important to him? Unsurprisingly, Brakes himself was just as displeased by Mayhew's interference if the tone of his voice was anything to go by.

"I'll let it go when I have answers." Brakes replied curtly, and Vera couldn't help but smile to herself at his answer.

Mayhew left soon after that, but the seed of irritation had already been planted within Brakes. She could feel the unsettling darkness roll off of him in waves and, despite wanting to ask if he was fine, Vera knew better. Sometimes, Brakes simply needed time to stew in his own thoughts before being asked silly questions.

After ten or so minutes since Mayhew had taken his leave, Vera heard the familiar scraping of Brakes' chair as he stood from his desk and turned to her.

"I'll be leaving for an hour or so, Vera," he murmured. Not bothering to look up from her paperwork, she offered him a nod. "It will be a late one today; be sure to rest when you can." A second later he was grabbing his trilby hat and coat and walking away, most likely taking a much-needed stroll into town before stopping by his favourite café. That was what he usually did when his mind could not settle.

Looking up from her work, Vera watched as Brakes retreated from the station. Once again, she wondered how she might be able to help him before considering if it was even possible for her to help him at all.

About fifteen minutes later, Vera finished off her paperwork and decided to join Brakes for a spot of tea. She thought that it would probably be a good idea to grab some food as well, considering the fact she would be working late again.

Grabbing the keys to her car, Vera picked up her hat and coat. Once she was outside, she took a deep breath. The fresh late afternoon air was a welcome change and once she had her fill of it, she headed straight for her car and made her way into the centre of Norwich.

Arriving at Brakes' favourite café, she parked right outside and immediately spotted her colleague sitting at his usual table situated outside of the establishment, quietly watching the world go by. Taking off her driving gloves, Vera left them on the dashboard and got out of the car to walk over to Brakes' table.

"Okay to join you, sir?" she asked, immediately breaking Brakes' concentration as he looked up and gave her a sharp nod.

"Of course, Vera," he said, gesturing to the chair across from him. "What can I get you?"

"Tea, and if they have some rabbit stew that would be lovely. Thank you, sir." Vera said, sitting down and offering Brakes a smile, one that he did not return. Instead, he waved over one of the café workers and placed Vera's order. Then his eyes wandered back towards the crowd of people that were walking through the city centre, going about their day despite the horrors of the war.

As she watched him, Vera could not help but consider that he seemed different, somehow. Almost lost, though not in the way he had seemed since the cold case had grown even colder. No, this sense of loss was wistful, almost, one that seemed to bring joy to his eyes.

She had not seen that look in a long time, not since they had discovered the parachutes had been sabotaged.

"Something brought a smile to your day, sir?" she asked, hoping that he might offer her an answer. Surprisingly, Brakes did smile at her question and returned his gaze to hers.

"Oh, just memories. It's a long story, Vera." he replied with a low chuckle and a shake of his head. "One that took place over a decade ago." And then he fell quiet again, a hand reaching for his jaw. As if deep in thought, Brakes began to rub a finger over his bottom lip, his gaze once again falling back to the crowd of people walking through the city centre.

"Well, I am eating, so I have the time," Vera offered brightly just as a café worker came with her tea and rabbit stew. "It would be an honour to listen to a story that seems to bring you joy, more so now when we seem to be surrounded by so much death and destruction. Please, share your thoughts, sir."

Pouring her tea, Vera watched as Brakes sighed deeply. He sat up in his seat and poured himself another cup of coffee.

"I was almost married once," he revealed slowly, and Vera's eyes lit up. "To my childhood sweetheart, in fact." Taking a sip of his coffee, Brakes nodded his head as Vera leaned in.

"Oh, how wonderful, sir!" she exclaimed brightly, but then she paused, her smile faltering. "So, what happened?"

For a moment Brakes was silent as he nursed his coffee, his gaze wandering off into the distance again. A wistful smile formed on his lips as he sat back in his seat and recalled the past.

"We met when we were fourteen years old and started stepping out after a month of two of friendship. Nothing serious, you understand. Just teenage stuff." He laughed a little at the memory and took another sip of coffee before continuing. "Anyway; Carol was living here with her aunt because her parents wanted her to school here in England. They were US born and lived in New York, you see. Some type of top management people, if I remember correctly."

Vera nodded. "International liaison: how very debonair of you, sir, I must say." Grinning, she took a spoonful of stew and felt its warmth seep through her immediately, calming and familiar.

Brakes shot her an agreeing smile and took out his wallet. Vera watched as he pulled out a photo that had been concealed and though it was slightly faded, she could clearly see from the black and white image that Carol's beauty was great. Her hair looked to be blonde, and she had wide, piercing eyes that would have undoubtedly penetrated one's soul if given the fortune of meeting her.

"A very beautiful woman, sir. A keeper for sure." Vera murmured as she stared down at the picture and the joy that had been so clearly captured in that moment. "Why did you let her go?"

She asked the question carefully, hoping that Brakes would not shut her out. Instead, he simply let out another sigh and returned the picture to his wallet.

"Oh, believe me; that decision was taken away from me a long time ago." Shaking his head, Brakes placed his wallet back into the pocket his coat and shrugged. "Anyway, today is the anniversary of our journey's end. This table, it... it was our table. We would spend hours here drinking tea and holding hands as if nothing else mattered in the world."

Dipping his finger into his coffee, Vera watched as Brakes did something she had never expected of him: He drew a heart on the table, the liquid staining the wood for a moment before slowly beginning to seep into the surface. Rubbing his fingers together, Brakes shook his head once again and closed his eyes.

"Another memory, sir?" she asked softly, pointing her spoon at the heart that would soon start fading.

Brakes nodded. "Winter or summer, I would always draw a sign of our love on this tabletop. The winter cold meant I didn't have to use tea or coffee every time." Brakes stopped for a moment and swallowed, as if even memories had flooded the forefront of his mind. "We kept each other warm whenever we were sat here, laughing and playing around, telling each other stories from our lives. We would always trace patterns or shapes on the table or even the pathway. Carol adored it, called it our silent language. If I could have spent every moment of the day with her, I would have."

Brakes' voice had fallen to a whisper, his gaze now set firmly on the heart he'd drawn onto the table. Nodding, Vera ate another spoonful of stew as she mulled over his words.

"Sounds like you found true love, sir."

Chuckling, Brakes nodded. "She was everything I had ever wanted, Vera. Yes, she was beautiful, but she was mischievous and had a bigger heart than anyone I knew. She understood me and my dreams, knew that I wanted something more than the predictable life mapped out for us in this city. She saw me in a way that no one else ever had."

Vera nodded, choosing to stay quiet in this rare personal moment with Brakes. He did not often show it, but he was a deeply caring soul, someone who was far more vulnerable than he dared to let on. Continuing to eat her stew, Vera waited for Brakes to speak again.

"I asked her to marry me one winters evening," he whispered. Vera held back a gasp. "I was taking her home. We had been tracing patterns in the snow. I'd been nervous all week, planning how I'd do it, what I would say. In the end, I don't think I needed to say anything. She would have said yes anyway, but she looked so beautiful that night, Vera. Almost ethereal."

"What did you say?" Vera asked, her voice barely above a whisper. At her question, Brakes' smile turned tender, his eyes softening.

"I told her that she was the sun in my sky and the north star that guides me. Then I got down on one knee and proposed." he explained gently before a hearty chuckle escaped him. "I couldn't feel my knees for an hour after that. It was bloody cold! But Carol said 'yes' the moment she laid eyes on the ring, and that was all that mattered."

Vera felt her eyes sting, the tell-tale prick of tears threatening to fall. Taking out her handkerchief, she quickly dabbed her eyes. "How romantic, sir," she murmured, noticing that even Brakes' eyes seemed to shine far more than usual, as if he too were on the brink of tears.

For a moment they sat together in silence to regain their composure. Taking out his own handkerchief, Vera watched as Brakes wiped his face before continuing.

"We spent the next few months planning the wedding. We argued a bit over cake flavours, of course, but we mostly focused on our future together. On us." Smiling mostly to himself, Brakes picked up his cooling coffee and took a sip. "We were very young, Vera. So young and hopelessly in love that we were utterly convinced our happiness was unbreakable."

Vera nodded and picked up her own cup of tea. "Is that when you decided to join the police, sir?" She asked. Brakes nodded.

"Yes. We talked about it at great length, and it was decided that joining the police would provide us with a solid foundation to build a great future on." Brakes explained.

As they talked, the café owner approached the table to clear away the plates before asking if they required anything else. Looking up at the man, Brakes shook his head. "No thank you, Harold."

Vera offered the café owner a smile before turning back to Brakes, who was now frowning as he looked into the distance.

"We were engaged for a year when she arrived at my parent's house one night. She was in a right state." he continued, his voice growing thick as Vera sat there, listening intently. "Carol's father had been diagnosed with cancer. He was a quiet man, stoic one might say, but he was everything to Carol. Told us the cancer was aggressive. She..." Brakes' words caught in his throat, and it took all Vera had in her to not reach over and take hold of his hand.

"Sir," she whispered, her eyes growing wide as the lines in Brakes' face grew even deeper, his face worn from the memories he was now reliving. "That is such a terrible thing, sir. I am so sorry."

"The wedding plans were immediately put on hold." Brakes continued, almost as if he hadn't heard her. "Carol booked the first flight to New York to be with him. It was the hardest thing I had to do, watching her leave me as I stood at the departure gate. I promised her that what we had was forever, that this separation was only temporary."

Brakes took a fortifying breath and began blinking rapidly, clearly fighting back his tears. Vera felt her breath catch in her throat; she had never once seen Brakes cry before today and yet here he was, close to tears for the second time that afternoon.

He continued. "Carol spent the next six months by her father's bedside. She watched him fade away. Watched as the man she had known succumbed to the disease that was eating away at him. I called every day, of course. I told her how much I missed her laughter, her warmth. I tried my hardest to bridge that distance, to keep the love and connection we had alive. But the ocean between us felt wider with each passing day."

"It must have been such a strain on everyone, sir." Vera whispered.

Brakes cleared his throat but did not answer her. Instead, he repositioned himself in his seat and finished his coffee.

"Her father died in the morning during autumn. He was surrounded by his loved ones, but it was a loss that deeply affected Carol and her mother. It suffocated them both." Brakes' voice had fallen to that of a whisper, his face growing pale as he relayed the details to Vera. Then, as if to punctuate his loss, a chill picked up in the air and Vera shuddered. "Carol's mother was always strong, the independent type. When her husband died, however, she was lost. Vulnerable. Carol couldn't leave her, not when the wounds of loss were still so fresh. A few nights after her father's passing, I got the phone call."

Vera knew what he was going to say next. There was nothing else he could say. Carol had chosen not to return, and a love that had once felt unbreakable had quickly become fragmented, the final thread ready to snap.

"She told me she couldn't come back. She felt so guilty, as if it were all her fault. But it wasn't. I could never blame my Carol." Brakes explained, a pang of sorrow in his voice. "I told her, 'I know, Carol. I understand.' And then she put the phone down on me for the last time."

Brakes paused, his eyes glistening in the low light of the falling sun as Vera watched him, still in her seat and clutching at her handkerchief. Then Brakes was shaking his head, his voice trembling.

"She wouldn't take my calls. I wrote to her several times, but no reply came. Eventually, I knew it was well and truly over."

Brakes looked away again, barely moving in his seat as he looked out at the city and the life that continued moving before them. Picking up her handkerchief, Vera sniffed and wiped her eyes again. She had never known Brakes to be the sort to have a sweetheart or to consider marriage. She had only known him as a detective, someone who ran headfirst into each case he came across. Now, she knew better. She knew that was just as human as she was and that he had suffered loss just as everyone else had.

"What a heartbreaking story, sir. I am so sorry." she whispered, lowering her gaze to her now lukewarm tea. "Though, it does answer one question that had puzzled me for a while."

Looking up, she watched as Brakes turned back to her with a raised brow.

"And what would that be, Vera?"

"Well, I always wondered why such a good-looking fella like yourself didn't have a woman in his life." she explained. Brakes huffed out a laugh, amused by her statement. "Even after ten years or more, you're still not over her. It's a truly beautiful thing and it brings warmth to my heart and a tear to my eyes."

She fell quiet after speaking and turned to look over at the city centre, watching as the sun sank lower on the horizon. She could hear Brakes sniff behind her and move in his chair, perhaps to wipe his own eyes, before he finally cleared his throat again and spoke up.

"Right. That's enough reminiscing for one day, Vera. It's time to get back to work," he muttered. She heard the chair scrape against the concrete behind her as he stood up.

Turning back to Brakes, Vera quickly finished off her tea and stood. Following Brakes to the car, she watched him perch his favourite hat on his head as he rounded the car to the passenger side. Before he opened the door, Brakes stared at her long and hard, his eyes once again holding a familiar determination that she had come to admire.

"You will soon come to realise that this job takes everything you have, Vera," he told her, his tone firm. "There isn't room for long-term relationships. Do well to remember that."

Sliding into his seat, Vera stood at the driver's side of the car for a moment as she took in his words, a frown forming on her lips. It had been a dream of hers to join the police, and working with Brakes had only made her desires stronger. Yet right now, it felt as if he was warning her away from the life she had been running towards.

Shaking her head, Vera put Brakes' words to the back her mind and got in the car.

CHAPTER SEVEN

Brakes had seen his fair share of crime, even before the war had turned the world upside down. But the nature of the crimes in Norwich had changed in recent months—the black market had become a festering sore on the city, a place where desperation and profiteering met in dark alleys and behind closed doors. People were hungry, rationing was strict, and ordinary goods had become valuable currency. Cigarettes, sugar, even tinned meat could fetch a high price. But it wasn't just food or luxury items disappearing now. Personal items—family heirlooms, jewellery, coins, and other valuables—were vanishing from bombed-out homes.

He had been investigating the black market for weeks, chasing down leads on smuggled goods and illegal ration trading. But the more he dug, the more he realised that these thefts weren't just crimes of opportunity committed by starving citizens. They were too coordinated, too precise. The victims reported that the items were gone almost as soon as the dust from the bombs had settled, and that raised a troubling possibility in Brakes' mind: What if those meant to help in times of crisis were actually the ones orchestrating the thefts?

Brakes pondered the possibility that either the local residents—or maybe The Air Raid Precaution (ARP) personnel—were filling their pockets. The first responders would be some of the first people on the scene whenever a bomb fell. They were supposed to be the guardians of the city, ensuring that people were safe and helping to salvage belongings from the wreckage and guiding the injured to safety. But what if, under the cover of chaos, some ARP members were helping themselves instead?

It was all speculation at this point, and it could be anyone, of course, so Brakes would need to speak to them all. Still, the pattern was clear, so much so that even a trainee could see it.

Brakes sat at his desk, a stack of reports regarding lost or stolen items of value piled in front of him, each one detailing a different victim's account. They had all been residents of areas recently hit by bombing raids. Their homes had been damaged or destroyed and, in the aftermath, as they struggled to pick up the pieces of what was left of their lives, they had noticed things were missing. Valuable things. At first, people assumed the items had been buried under debris or worse, looted by the lowest of people—scavengers preying off the dead.

Any bombed-out house or street was considered unsafe until the fire brigade told people otherwise. No one was allowed to approach, not even the victims' families. They had to wait to retrieve their loved ones. Of course, many people simply took no notice and regardless of the danger, they searched for those they had lost, regrettably sometimes in vain.

When Brakes and Vera had spoken to the victim's family members, the stories regarding the local fire brigade, the police and the ARP only became more and more unsettling. Each person had recalled how the local residents had said that the Brigades and the ARP men were generally first on the scene and how they had been helpful and efficient, sometimes overly so.

They'd offered to take care of things, telling the distraught residents to go to shelters or rest while they managed the wreckage. Those who had lost their homes in the carnage were told that it would be made safe for them to return, that the local services would attempt to salvage what they could. Most times it took days, and no one could really say how many people had actually passed through the wreckage during that time.

When the homeowners returned, they would have been directed towards a makeshift lost and found. After that, a small percentage of people reported that their prized possessions—mainly jewellery or small items that would be quick and easy to sell on—were gone, lost to the horrors of war.

That was the sad reality of it all, of course; many of these items had in fact been used in trades. Trinkets were used to barter for black market goods, heirlooms carelessly traded for meat, dairy and tinned foods, all stolen from who knows where. Of course, that begged the question of just who the main benefactor was at the end of this immoral triangle.

It was simple, really. It was those who already had everything. While the everyday person worked and struggled to make ends meet and feed their families, it was the rich who were buying, bartering and trading with the morally corrupt. Thus, the wealthy were able to host the most lavish of dinner parties and continue their extravagant lifestyles.

To Brakes, it was clear as day that the people who were supposed to protect the vulnerable were, in fact, aiding the rich in their corrupt dealings, perhaps even benefitting from it in some way, too. Sadly, Brakes knew that unfounded accusations made regarding any of the home front personnel would be met with dire results.

The Fire brigade, Police and ARP were respected, even revered for their bravery and tireless work during the bombings. Accusing them of theft—especially organised theft—would rattle the city to its core. So, Brakes and Vera would have to tread carefully, and he especially would need to keep his mouth shut while the knowledge of the home front personnel's corruption ate away at him.

As Brakes read through another report, his thoughts were interrupted by a familiar voice from behind him.

"Thinking about the ARP or the Fire Brigade are you, sir?" Vera asked, perching herself on the edge the desk. She had a way of knowing what was on Brakes' mind without him saying a word. Even though Vera was Brakes' driver, there was no denying that she had become more than that since they had first met. Sharp-witted, observant and always ready with a dry remark, she had an uncanny ability to cut through to the heart of a matter, often offering insights that Brakes couldn't help but grudgingly appreciate.

"I am," Brakes replied, not looking up from the file in front of him. "Too many coincidences. Every one of these thefts happens right after a raid, and every victim mentions the area is swarming with people. There is just no path to follow at this point—it could be any one person or a gang. I'm totally at a loss, Vera."

Leaning over, Vera rifled through the reports he had meticulously organised. She had an air of casual disregard for authority that Brakes found both infuriating and oddly refreshing. Where he was methodical, she was instinctive and while he would never admit it, her instincts were often annoyingly accurate.

"Well, first on the scene are the Brigades and the ARP, correct?" she said, flipping through one of the reports. "They're the ones running in when everyone else is running out."

"That's exactly the problem," Brakes muttered, his voice low. "They're trusted, so no one questions them. But what if that trust is being abused?"

Vera raised an eyebrow. "You're saying the Brigade or the ARP are thieves now?"

Brakes leaned back in his chair, rubbing a hand over his tired eyes. "Not outside of this conversation I'm not, no. And you will never repeat that to anyone, Vera."

Vera considered this for a moment before nodding slowly. "I've heard worse theories. We're going to need proof. Solid, unquestionable proof." Tapping her foot against the desk, Vera looked at Brakes with a grin. "So, what are you going to do about it?"

Brakes hadn't quite figured that part out yet. He couldn't just walk into the police, Fire or ARP's respective headquarters and start throwing around accusations. He needed proof, something concrete to back up his suspicions. And that was the difficult part.

"These men are smart, careful. They wouldn't leave evidence behind. They certainly wouldn't leave stolen goods in plain sight, either." Brakes stated, his tone even. Vera nodded. "We will have to approach this carefully. It would be great if we could place one of our own with them."

"It can't be one of us, sir. You are too well known," Vera added unhelpfully, as if Brakes hadn't thought of that already. "And since last year, wherever you went, I was right there beside you."

Brakes nodded idly. Vera was right—they were both quite recognisable thanks to their efforts the year prior, Brakes more so due to his time with the police. If only he could use his trilby hat as a disguise, or apply some makeup so he might appear different...

Sitting upright in his seat, his eyes immediately met with Vera's. That was it!

"Oh, Vera, it seems you have forgotten an important fact," he said, his smile widening as Vera looked at him curiously. "You ladies have an unbelievable power, one that you train for over many years."

Vera's eyebrows rose and she folded her arms across her chest. "Sir, I am sure I have no idea what you are talking about."

"You ladies have the ability to look totally different by simply changing your clothes, hair colour, makeup, even by simply putting a hat on. You've been doing it for years—dressing up, playing different parts. How different would it be to change you appearance a little bit and place you in another brigade?" Jumping up from his seat, Brakes grabbed Vera by the arm and pulled her to a standing position. "Come on, Vera! Don't tell me you're not up for this? It's a genius idea!"

At his excitement, Vera couldn't help but smile too and gave Brakes an equally enthusiastic nod in agreement.

"I must agree, sir; it is a brilliant idea, quite possibly one of your best."

With her approval, Brakes immediately left his desk to go run the idea by the Chief. He had expected some pushback, but surprisingly the talk went easier than anticipated.

"I think it is a good idea, Brakes," the Chief told him once Brakes had given him a rundown of the idea. "Though I must insist that you keep a close eye on Constable Stanshore. Please, keep her as safe as you possibly can."

Heading back to his desk, Brakes was met with a very excitable Vera, who was practically jumping up and down on the spot like a giddy schoolgirl.

"What did he say?" She asked, bouncing up to him with a gleam in her eyes. "Did he say yes, sir? Did he say yes?"

Shaking his head, Brakes placed a hand on Vera's shoulder in a bid to calm her down. Though it was clear that she was still trembling with anticipation, Vera calmed herself enough to still beneath Brakes' palm as he looked her straight in the eye.

"Calm yourself, Vera," he instructed her, his voice low and even. "To answer your question, yes; the Chief has said yes to the operation." At his confirmation, Vera's breath hitched and her smile widened greatly, her body practically vibrating from the excitement of it all. Before she could begin jumping again, Brakes lifted a finger with his free hand and looked at her sternly. "But he has insisted we be subtle. Can you do that, Vera?"

At his question, Vera could barely hold back her glee. "The real question is if can you be subtle, sir? Now, that I'd like to see."

Huffing in annoyance at her cheek, Brakes gave her a stern look, but there was no malice behind it. Vera always had a way of lightening the mood, even when the weight of the job felt suffocating. He appreciated her irreverence, though he'd never admit it to her face.

"You'd be surprised," he replied dryly. "Sometimes I can be quite charming."

Vera laughed, a sharp, quick sound that filled the room. "I'll take your word for it, sir."

CHAPTER EIGHT

Once it had been confirmed that Vera would operate as a double agent, it was decided that she should join the ARP, and so both Brakes and Vera took off to requisition some much-needed clothing. It would be easy enough to insert Vera into this new role, one that would allow her to keep an eye on most of the people around her, including the Fire Brigade.

Upon returning to the station, Vera took herself to the ladies' room to change. Ten or so minutes later, Vera reappeared wearing a black tunic and skirt. Her hair was down, and she now adorned a black helmet with a white 'W' on the front.

"I'm ready, sir. What do you think?" she asked, turning on the spot while Brakes appraised her new look.

"You certainly look the part, Vera," Brakes agreed, nodding as she stopped turning and beamed. "Now, listen to me; under no circumstances should you take any chances to catch or even attempt to arrest anyone on your own. You are there to gather evidence, and evidence only. There will be no heroics or shenanigans that can potentially disrupt the operation. Do you understand?"

Standing to attention, Vera tilted her chin and looked Brakes square in the eye as she gave him an agreeing nod.

"Yes, sir, don't worry, sir. I won't let you down."

Now all they had to do was wait for the perfect opportunity to rise that would enable Vera to infiltrate the ARP. Of course, that all depended on if the Third Reich remembered their role in the war, and soon.

The opportunity to test this rouse came sooner than expected. That same night as the air raid sirens wailed their shrill warning across Norwich, Brakes and Vera were already in the car making their way through the darkened streets toward the area where bombs had reportedly fallen. The blacked-out city was eerie at night, the only light coming from the faint glow of fires in the distance or the occasional flash of searchlights scanning the skies.

They arrived in a neighbourhood that had been hit hard—rows of terraced houses reduced to smouldering rubble, the acrid smell of burning wood and brick dust filling the air. The ARP crews were already on the scene, their gas masks hanging loosely around their necks as they moved through the destruction, calling out for survivors and marking buildings deemed too dangerous to enter.

Donned in her ARP uniform, it was easy enough for Vera to slip in amongst the other ARP officials and begin assisting them in their work while Brakes watched from a distance.

His sharp eyes scanned their movements as the ARP helped to usher people out of the area. To the untrained observer, everything looked normal. The ARP men were doing their jobs—clearing debris, guiding people to safety, checking for fires. But Brakes wasn't looking for what was obvious. He was looking for what wasn't.

"Seen anything?" Vera muttered when she passed him with a walking victim, her breath fogging in the cool night air.

"Not yet," Brakes murmured, tipping the rim of his hat low over his face. "But keep your eyes on them. Especially if they go inside any houses."

Vera gave a small, barely-there nod before passing him as she continued to help the ARP men while they moved through the wreckage. Brakes was certain that her sharp eyes would catch each miniscule detail, cataloguing everything to report back to him once she was done. As time ticked on, her once immaculate uniform was now covered in dust and patches of blood. Much like everyone else, she soon bore her own wounds, her knees, arms and chin scraped open as she ran through the barbed wire.

It took several hours before the only people left on the street were the Fire and ARP personnel. Thankfully, it seemed as if the death toll this time around was small, with most people making it to their designated air raid shelters. Once all the fires had been put out, Brakes knew that it was time for the Fire Brigade and ARP to start the grim task of searching through the rubble one last time.

The air, despite still being thick with smoke and unsettled dust, did not stop some people lighting up a cigarette, an action that caused Vera's nose to crinkle in disgust Brakes noticed even from afar.

Turning his gaze away from Vera's ministrations, Brakes noted the tea ladies who had set up a table just a few short strides away from the danger zone. Now a common practice after an air raid, these ladies would arrive once the injured or dead had been removed and setup a makeshift table where pots of tea were served. With their unwavering smiles—and sometimes the odd biscuit, though they never lasted long—these women offered a source of comfort and warmth to the gruelling personnel.

Yet Brakes knew that there was more to it than the tea ladies offering a spot of positivity during a trying time. Despite the British stiff upper lip mentality, the tea ladies' mere presence conveyed a powerful message to everyone around them: '*We will never* surrender', or in more colloquial terms, *'Up yours, Hitler.'*

As some members of the Fire and ARP personnel made their way to the table and drank tea, others would start treating their own cuts. Eventually, some of the wives and sweethearts of frontline men came to their aid. A few of them ripped clean sheets into strips and used them as makeshift bandages, while others formed in neat lines to help remove the rubble brick by brick, their determination and spirit unwavering.

By daybreak, it was as if an army had infiltrated the scene. Much like any other bomb site, regardless of the town or city, people banded together. It was an inspiring sight, one that reminded Brakes of the camaraderie people held, even in the throes of war.

And yet, despite how warm of a scene it looked, it was one that did not answer Brakes' question. Were the home front personnel truly corrupt, just as he suspected, or was he wrong? He had come here to find answers, but it seemed that those very answers were intent on alluding him.

As the sun continued to rise and even more people came to offer their help, Brakes knew that it was time to leave. Almost begrudgingly, he signalled for Vera to follow him out of the area.

Once they were out of sight, he took Vera by the elbow and pulled her close. "We've done all that we can here," he murmured, his voice low in case anyone passed them. "Besides, there are far too many people around for anyone to do anything dishonest. Let's go get cleaned up."

He pulled at her arm in a bid to leave, only for Vera to stand firm. Sighing, Brakes removed his hand and turned to her with a questioning look. She was frowning, her gaze returning to the bomb site as her brows pinched together in contemplation.

"Maybe that's the point, sir. Maybe the people have had enough and are now looking out for each other more than ever." Vera replied gently, her gaze softening as she watched even more people arrive to help. After a minute of watching the scene before her, she finally lifted her shoulders in a solemn shrug and turned on her heel as Brakes quickly followed suit.

It took about ten minutes for them to drive to the station. The city of Norwich was already in full swing as they drove by, the people going about their daily chores as if nothing had happened under the cover of darkness that very morning.

Upon arriving at the station, they both parted ways to clean up before Vera went to off to the communal area to make them two cups of coffee. Sitting heavily in his chair, Brakes waited at his desk as uniformed officers passed by, offering him a polite 'Hello' before returning to their own desks. Finally, after what felt like a lifetime, Vera shuffled past a few people with two steaming cups in her hand.

They sat in silence. They were both undoubtedly worn out and for Brakes especially, dismayed by their lack of progress. Taking a sip of his coffee, he took off his hat to run a hand through his hair.

Vera spoke first. "It wasn't a total wash out, sir." she offered cheerfully, though her voice seemed a little more wilted than usual. "We did help a lot of people this morning. We can at least take some solace in that."

Brakes knew that she was right. They had done a good thing that night, even if their mission had yielded fewer answers than he would have liked.

"I agree, Vera, it's just..." Sighing deeply, Brakes set his cup down on the desk and shook his head. "One can't help but wonder if it will ever end. How many lives must be lost because of one man's disturbing vision of the world? When will someone finally have the guts to say that's enough?"

Pushing his chair back, Brakes picked up his coffee cup again and lifted his feet until they were resting on the desk. Taking a long, thoughtful sip, he rested his head against the back of his chair and closed his eyes.

Vera said nothing in response, instead choosing to finish her own coffee while Brakes considered their next move. If the ARP and Fire Brigade were truly corrupt, then how might they navigate a situation with so many eyes on them?

After several minutes, Brakes set his now empty coffee cup down and swung his legs off the desk. Jumping from his seat with renewed vigour, he looked to Vera with determined eyes. "Right. Let's go and see if we can ruffle a few feathers, Vera. You okay to bring the car round?"

Setting down her own cup, Vera nodded eagerly. "Sure am, sir. Where are we off to, then?" she asked.

"We're paying a visit to both the ARP and Fire stations," Brakes grinned, grabbing his coat and putting on his trilby hat as Vera stood, her eyes shining with excitement.

"I'll get the car," she said, then hesitated before adding, "I just need to visit the ladies' room on my way out."

Nodding, Brakes made his way through the station and outside where he waited patiently for Vera. Surprisingly, it took some time for her to appear with the car, but when she finally arrived Brakes understood why—she was now wearing her police uniform with her hair pulled back.

Sliding into the car, they set off to their first stop: the ARP station.

Upon arrival, Brakes could see three men huddled around a barrel of fire set in an arched metal building. Materials were scattered around it, including wood to make signs, shovels, pickaxes and a whole host of other tools that were presumably used by the men in the cause of their duties. Stepping out of the car, Brakes made sure that Vera stood close behind him.

As they approached, one of the men looked up. Rising from his seat, he turned to his comrades and announced their presence with a booming voice.

"Oi! We have visitors!"

It was as if everyone turned at once, their beady eyes locking onto Brakes and Vera as they stepped forward. Reaching into his coat pocket, Brakes took out his identification.

"DI Brakes and Constable Stanshore, Norwich constabulary." he stated loudly as the men's gaze flickered between his identification papers and his face. Once he was certain they believed who he was, Brakes withdrew his hand as one of the men stepped forward, clearly wary of their appearance.

"What can we do for you, then?" he asked, his gaze sliding over to Vera who stood behind Brakes. "We're just about to head home. We've had a busy night, you see."

"Yes, we are aware. We were there," Vera blurted out, and immediately the men all turned their gazes to her. Sighing to himself, Brakes shot Vera a pointed look over his shoulder to keep quiet. Closing her mouth, Vera offered him a subtle nod as he turned back to the men, all of whom were still carefully watching Vera with heightened interest.

Clearing his throat, Brakes hoped to draw their attention back to him. "So, who are you gentlemen, then?" he asked. Thankfully, the first man turned back to Brakes, his mouth twisting into an unimpressed frown.

"I'm Frankie. I am in charge of this bunch of misfit rabble," the man replied gruffly as he wiped his palms on his jacket sleeves. Then he was pointing to the man closest to him who was still eyeing Vera almost appreciatively. "This is Tony, and the young'un over there is Mikey." Then he was grinning, his gaze locked onto Brakes'. "So, to what do we owe the pleasure of your visit, Inspector?"

Drawing a breath, Brakes stepped forward. "There has been a spate of thefts from the bombed-out buildings around the city." he explained, keeping his tone even. Immediately, this caught the other two men's attention, and they both turned to look at him. "I would like to stress that I am not accusing anyone of anything, of course, however I would like to know if you have been made aware of any thefts or know anything about them. Anything at all."

Falling silent, he watched each of them for their reaction, anything that might hint at their involvement or knowledge. It was the younger one of the bunch who moved first, instantly turning his head to glance up at Frankie. Only his face was out of Brakes' view, and Frankie

didn't seem to show any hint of a reaction, either. Tony, on the other hand, simply sipped his tea while turning his gaze back to the fire in front of him.

Silence permeated around them, the crackle of the flames filling the space as Vera shuffled awkwardly on the spot behind Brakes. Shaking his head, Brakes considered that a different approach might work in his favour.

"It was one hell of a night last night, hey, fella's." he said, his lips curling into an easy smile. "I have to be honest, that was my first time at the aftermath of a bombing. It almost seems like controlled, well-rehearsed chaos, to be fair."

Eyeing him warily, Frankie twisted his neck and spat on the ground. As if on cue, Tony looked up from the fire and for the first time since meeting them, Brakes noticed that the man seemed to suffer from an eye twitch, something that could be the result of anxiety or perhaps a lack of sleep.

"We all have our jobs to do. We just get on with it and do the best we can," Tony replied, his voice low and gravelly. "We're here to help people, not steal from them."

Making sure to meet Tony's eye, Brakes stood firm and straightened his posture. "Again, we are only here to ask if you gents have seen anything suspicious at any time whilst on duty." he reiterated, though it did not seem to calm the men down any less. In fact, it only seemed to irritate Frankie and Tony more.

Instead of answering him, Frankie instead turned to Tony, his voice low as they spoke in whispers. Brakes took this moment of quiet to look around the building, though he was sure to keep an eye on the men. Of course, he knew that Vera would be ever vigilant in watching them, too.

It seemed that the youngest of the men, Mikey, was intent on watching his elders, however.

Taking off his hat, Brakes stepped closer to the fire and started twisting the fedora in his hands as he turned to the lad. "Have you been in the ARP long, Mikey? You don't look like you have many cuts or bruises," he said and jerked his head in Vera's direction. "My poor constable over there is cut to shreds from all the sharp edges last night."

Mikey looked up in alarm, surprised that Brakes was addressing him. Hesitantly, he glanced over at Frankie and Tony again, both of whom were still in the throes of quiet conversation. Turning back to Vera and Brakes, the young lad drew in a deep breath before speaking up.

"A couple of months," he said carefully and swallowed hard, almost as if there was a lump caught in his throat. "I'm flat footed so couldn't join up. I decided to join the ARP instead."

As Mikey said this, both Frankie and Tony looked up again, their focus unnervingly on Vera now. With a leering glance, Tony's eyes roved over the length of Vera's body as he took a sip of tea and said, "You wanna give us a look at *your* battle scars then, sweety?"

"You stand a better chance of having dinner with the King," Vera replied glibly, her eyes steely and cold as she glared back at Tony, whose eye seemed to twitch even more violently, now.

Surprise flashed across both Frankie and Mikey's features as Brakes coughed into his hand to disguise a rising chuckle. He was well aware that Vera could hold her own of course, but these men had been caught unaware.

Shooting Vera a small smile, Brakes quickly turned back to the men to see Frankie glaring at Tony before steepling his fingers together and moving toward his seat.

"We'll keep a look out and let you know if we see anything, Inspector," he grunted, falling into his seat and picking up a cup of tea. "Now, if you don't mind, we are all tired and need to get some sleep. Good day."

Turning away from them, Frankie started drinking his tea when Brakes cleared his throat again, this time much louder.

"Just one last thing, Frankie," Brakes said, earning a look of annoyance from the man as he turned to look back at him. "Please provide my Constable with your full names and addresses. Once that is done, we will be on our way and leave you to your day."

Begrudgingly, Frankie and his men recited their information to Vera while Brakes continued to study them closely. Finally, when their information was recorded in Vera's notebook, they bid the men a good day and headed for the car.

Putting her gloves on, Vera started the car and asked, "The Fire station next then, sir?"

Brakes shook his head. "No. Let's go to the café first, Vera. We'll grab a coffee and a bite to eat." Slinging his hat onto the backseat, Brakes took out his notebook and started jotting things down as Vera nodded and drove away.

When they arrived at the café, the duo immediately sat at Brakes' favourite table and ordered some sandwiches and a pot of tea to share, as the establishment had run out of coffee. Once it arrived, Brakes noted how much brighter Vera seemed as she set to pouring them both a cup each. Perhaps she was not a fan of coffee like he was?

"What are your thoughts on the ARP fellows, sir?" Vera asked, handing him a cup of hot tea before pouring her own. At her question, Brakes sat back in his seat and pondered on their interaction with the three men.

"Well, Vera, it could be that much like us, they are tired. Exhaustion can make people twitchy, as you may know." Tilting his head, Brakes picked up his cup and looked into his tea. "That said, we can't eliminate them from our enquiries just yet. We will possibly have to revisit them at a later date and when we do, we should interview the younger one, Mikey, alone. Out of the three, he is the weak link."

"You think that he will be the easiest to break under interrogation?" Vera asked, her eyebrows rising. "That is, if they are hiding anything at all, sir."

Taking a sip of his tea, Brakes nodded. "Yes. He was constantly looking at the other two for validation." he pointed out. Placing his cup down, he took a generous bite out of his corned beef sandwich which had just arrived at their table.

They spent the next forty minutes finishing their lunch and watching the daily activities unfold around them in peace. Once they were done, Brakes paid the bill and thanked the owner for their lunch while Vera went to start the car. Pulling his coat closed, Brakes made his way over to the vehicle and jumped in.

"Let's visit the Fire station now, Vera," he said as she pulled away from the café. "Oh, and it might be a good idea for us to visit the known local movers afterwards."

"Movers, sir? Are you thinking of moving home?"

"No, Vera. It's another term used for 'fence'. You know, people who transport the product before selling it on. It's more of a street term than a police one to be honest."

"Are there many movers in Norwich then, sir?"

"There are two main players with a few on the lower rungs of the ladder. They're jumping around the board, hustling for position, waiting to be kinged. Just like in a game of draughts." Brakes explained.

"Who are the main players, then?" asked Vera.

"Well, down near the docks there is Derek Johnson, also known as *The Sea Serpent,* so called because most of his stock comes from ships. He also has several old warehouses dotted around Norwich, one of which I am sure is his HQ." Brakes stared out the window, his brow furrowing as they passed smouldering buildings and people desperately searching through the debris. "Then there is Brian Faulkner, also known as *The Grifter.* He cut his bones down in London, swindling and stealing from the rich. He owns several factories in and around Norwich, most of which are working on government contracts due to the war. He comes across as a reputable businessman and although we have never been able to prove anything, he is as dirty as they come."

Gripping the steering wheel, Vera nodded as she turned a corner and raced down the road.

"I am guessing that due to the high-end price tags of the stolen goods, these two are the only ones with the required funds to handle this type of loot then, sir?" Vera asked, her gaze sliding over to Brakes before quickly turning back to the road.

"Correct, Vera. But we will have to catch the fence with their hand in the till, so to speak," he said evenly, his eyes narrowing just as Vera pulled up in front of the fire station. Jumping out of the car,

Brakes glanced over at the building before turning back to the vehicle.

"Move a little further down, Vera, so as not to block the entrance. I will meet you in there soon." he instructed. With a quick nod, Vera drove further ahead as Brakes turned back to the building and strode towards the entrance.

As it turned out, the night staff had already left, meaning that Brakes had hit a brick wall. Begrudgingly, he took down the names and addresses of everyone that had worked that night before stalking back out of the station to find Vera walking towards the entrance, her eyes growing wide with surprise as she saw him leave.

"Total waste of time, Vera," he growled, one hand reaching for his hat as he stopped in front of her. "The night staff have gone home, but I have their names and addresses. We'll catch up with them later."

"Okay, sir," Vera said with a curt nod. "Back to the station, then?"

Shaking his head, Brakes began walking towards the car as Vera followed, quickly falling into step with him. "No. Let's call it a day. You can drop me off at the Bell to meet Doug for that beer I promised him. You can join us if you wish?"

Twisting his neck to look at her, he saw that Vera was shaking her head, a small smile curving on her lips.

"Not tonight, sir. Besides, it's a little early for the Bell; they don't open until 17:30 hours." Checking her watch, Vera walked around the car and opened the door to the driver's seat. "I also have my sister visiting me. We are going to take in a show at the theatre tonight."

Sliding into the passenger seat, Brakes checked his own watch for the time. "Oh, yes. You are quite right indeed, Vera." he replied, removing his hat and setting it on the dashboard. "You may drop me at the market square, then. I will do a little light shopping and wander up to the Bell afterwards."

"Understood, sir," replied Vera as she struck up the engine.

CHAPTER NINE

By the time Brakes and Doug left the bell the night prior, it was closing time, and they had certainly had their fair share of beer. Luckily for Brakes, Doug had a driver on standby to return him to the base, so they dropped Brakes off en route.

For the first time in months, Brakes took to fettling with his Triumph motorbike for a couple of hours before heading off to bed.

Brakes had not been asleep for long, the shrill ring of the phone piercing through the darkness, rousing him from a restless sleep. He had been dreaming, though the details quickly slipped away as he groped for the receiver and glanced at the clock. It was 04:40.

"Brakes here," he said, his voice thick with sleep but already hardening into the brisk tone of a professional investigator.

"DI Brakes, another body had been found, sir," came the voice of Constable Davies, a Suffolk officer Brakes had spoken to before. The urgency in his voice was unmistakable. "Same as the others. Parachute not deployed, looks like a civilian for sure because this person isn't dressed in military uniform, sir."

Brakes bolted upright, now fully awake. His pulse quickened, his mind already racing as the details sank in. This was what Brakes had been waiting for and what he expected would come sooner or later. The sixth body. Another victim in this bizarre pattern of deaths.

"Where is it?" Brakes asked, already swinging his legs out of bed and reaching for his trousers.

"In a woodland near Framlingham," replied Davies. "Same odd details. Found by a farmer heading out to check his livestock. As per the instructions given out in the alert, we have not touched anything and our medical officer is awaiting your arrival, sir. "

"I'm on my way," Brakes said, his voice tight. He hung up and was already on his feet, pulling on his shirt and trousers. Yanking on his overcoat and grabbing his fedora, Brakes almost knocked over the half-empty cup of cold tea left over from the night before in his excitement.

He hadn't expected it to come tonight. But the truth was he had been waiting for months, bracing himself for the moment when he would get the call that would break open the case or bury it even deeper in confusion.

Reaching for the phone again, he rang Vera.

"Pack an overnight bag and come get me," he said quickly, barely waiting for Vera's groggy reply. "There's been another murder by parachute. Come immediately, Vera."

The early morning air outside his cottage was crisp, still heavy with the chill of early spring. The outskirts of Norwich were quiet, with only the distant rumble of an airplane engine overhead hinting at the war that pressed in on every corner of the country.

Vera was always punctual, and this morning was no different. She stood by the black Wolseley police car, her black police uniform contrasting with the early morning fog, her cap positioned just so on her light brown hair. She looked calm, but there was an underlying alertness in her eyes that told Brakes she was fully awake and ready to go.

"Another one, you say?" Vera asked, her voice steady but filled with curiosity as Brakes threw a small bag on the back seat and then climbed into the passenger seat.

"Yeah. Parachute not deployed, except there is no military uniform this time. The victim was dress in civilian clothing." Brakes explained, fastening his seatbelt. "I'm afraid we have a bit of a drive this time, Vera."

"Where to then, sir?" she asked.

"Suffolk this time. Framlingham, to be exact."

Vera nodded. Pulling on her gloves, she placed her hands firmly on the wheel as she started the engine and pulled away. The Wolseley hummed to life, and they sped down the road, the fog rolling over the countryside like a ghostly blanket. Brakes stared out the window as they drove, his mind ticking over the details he knew and those he didn't.

Brakes gave himself a quick recap in his head. Whoever was behind these killings had taken their time. The bodies had been spread out over the years, each discovery isolated by distance and circumstance. Each victim had been found far from home, far from their natural environments, dressed in uniforms that didn't belong to them and saddled with a parachute that had never been used.

And now, another one. The sixth body. Except this time, they weren't dressed in a uniform. Whatever could that mean? Was it a message, or simply an error in the murderers' plans, Brakes wondered.

The drive down would take a few hours, so Brakes took this opportunity to continue their conversation from the café.

"So, tell me, Vera; what of you and love?" he asked.

"That's a very short story, sir," replied Vera, her lips forming into something akin to a smirk as opposed to her usual smile.

Brakes turned to look at her, his eyes growing wide. "Come on, Vera; you're young! And forgive me for saying this, but you are a beautiful lady. You must have the men lining up." Brakes exclaimed, watching as Vera desperately shook her head while focusing on the road ahead. "Don't think I haven't noticed that, everywhere we go, men steal more than just a glance at you."

"Oh, sir, please stop; you will make me blush," Vera mumbled, her cheeks already flushed pink. "Of course, there have been a few suitors, but nothing that would come anywhere close to your own experience."

"There is time yet, Vera. You have youth and your looks, and not forgetting that sharp mind of yours. It won't be long before you have the right man on your arm, begging for your affections." Brakes grinned teasingly, watching as Vera's face grew even redder while she tried desperately to ignore him.

They both fell into a momentary silence as they drove, the countryside passing them by. Eventually, it was Vera who broke it first.

"What's the plan once we arrive, sir?"

"We will grab the kit from the boot of the car; you take statements from whoever found the body and send them away as soon as you can. The less people we have around the better."

Vera nodded. "Okay, sir. Let's get there and get this done, then." she replied.

By the time they arrived in Framlingham, the sun was beginning to rise, but the fog still clung to the trees in thick swirls. The scene was eerily quiet as they pulled up to the edge of the forest where the body had been discovered. Several constables were already there, keeping a respectful distance from the body, which lay in the underbrush beneath the towering trees.

Brakes stepped out of the car, opened the boot and gathered their equipment. With Vera close behind, he strode toward the scene with great determination. The smell of damp earth and pine needles filled the air, mingling with the scent of smoke from a nearby chimney.

"Morning, sir. Detective Sergeant Miles," stated one of the men onsite. Stepping forward, he held out his hand for Brakes to shake. Ignoring the gesture, Brakes simply passed him by, his focus squarely on the victim that lay ahead.

"DI Brakes," he replied simply. Jerking his head in Vera's direction, he continued to make his way over to where the body had been found. "And this is Constable Stanshore. Would you be so kind as to point her towards the person that found him?"

Letting his hand fall, the man called Miles frowned at Brakes' demeanour. Pointing over to a group of officers, he turned on his heel and stalked off with Vera in tow, leaving Brakes to take in the grisly scene that awaited him.

The victim lay sprawled on his back while the unopened parachute lay tangled beneath him. His arms were splayed awkwardly at his sides, his clothing torn and barely hiding the deep-cut wounds that were on display. His head was turned slightly to the left, his face pale and gaunt, and Brakes could clearly see the heavy bruising and cuts that covered most of his skin. Just like he had been told, the victim was not dressed in military uniform.

As he looked over the latest victim, Brakes found it difficult to determine if any of the trauma shown had been inflicted prior to the man's fall. It was obvious that he had taken several hits from the tree branches as he sped through the canopy, but any other wounds could have easily been made prior to the fall.

While he studied the body, a uniformed officer made his way over to Brakes with another person in tow.

"You must be Detective Inspector Brakes. Constable Davies, sir. I was the one that phoned you this morning." Davies said in greeting, his face grim. "This is our medical officer onsite today, Doctor Baker."

Brakes offered them both a nod in response, though his focus was still on the body that lay mangled before him. He could not help but feel a flicker of excitement bubble within him, his sense of purpose once again renewed with the latest addition to a case that had only grown colder over the past year.

"What are your findings, Constable?" Brakes murmured, not once taking his eyes off the body. Beside him, he heard the distinctive rustle of paper as Davies flipped through his notebook.

"Factory worker," Davies said. "Name's Alfred Pearce. Mid-thirties. No military record, just like the others. His identification and work card were half out of his back pocket, sir. Here they are."

Davies proceeded to hand Brakes everything he had. Briefly flipping through the papers, Brakes nodded before crouching beside the body, studying the details. The parachute was intact, as expected, but the static line had clearly been tampered with beforehand, and nothing else. Brakes' eyes lingered on the victim's hands, which were calloused and rough—consistent with his work in the factory.

"What can you tell me, Doctor?" Looking up at the medical officer, Brakes stood to meet his eye level as the doctor frowned, his gaze falling to the mangle of limbs before him.

"Well, it's clear he hit several branches prior to impact. If you look closely, you can see tree bark and leaves imbedded in most of the wounds. His thoracic cage has totally collapsed, most likely from the impact. His head, limbs and torso have also suffered major trauma, some of which may well have killed him. Due to the extent of the injuries, it would be very difficult to determine what the cause of death was." The doctor explained, his words coming out rapidly as Brakes took it all in, memorising each new piece of information that now added to a case he had been chasing for so long.

Clapping a hand on the man's shoulder, Brakes gave him a firm nod. "Do the best you can, doctor. Once you have finished your report, please send it and his clothing directly to me at the Norwich police station." Brakes requested before turning back to the crime scene and taking in his surroundings.

From where he stood, Brakes could clearly see Mr. Pearce's path through the trees. Shaking his head in bewilderment, he turned to look for Vera, only to find that she was now a few paces away from him as she spoke with the doctor, her voice low. She was scribbling in her notebook, taking down statements as he had asked.

"What's your take, Vera?" Brakes asked, turning back to the victim once she had finished. As the doctor left, Vera knelt beside the body, her sharp eyes scanning the scene.

"Nothing different stands out, sir." Vera replied, her lips curling into a frown. Brakes nodded. The scene of the crime looked almost identical to the ones before now, almost as if it were an accident. The killer—or killers—were methodical. Each of these deaths had been planned, right down to the smallest detail. But why? What connected these people? A factory worker, a nurse, a butcher's daughter, an RAF mechanic... there didn't seem to be any logical link between them, yet they had all met the same fate.

As Brakes stood and surveyed the scene some more, his mind raced through the possibilities. It was clear that this wasn't the work of an amateur or some random psychopath. Whoever was responsible had access to military uniforms and equipment. They were precise, careful, and they were sending a message— but what that message was, remained maddeningly elusive.

As the sun rose higher in the sky, its light touching the harrowing scene before him, Brakes knew that the evidence they had simply wasn't enough. No, they needed more.

CHAPTER TEN

Back at the local constable's station, Brakes poured over the victim's file. Alfred Pearce, a local factory worker, unmarried and lived alone in a small, rented a flat on the edge of town. No known enemies, no signs of trouble at work. The factory where he worked produced parts for military vehicles, but other than that, there was nothing out of the ordinary about his life.

Vera sat across from him, flipping through her own notes.

"It doesn't add up," she said, tapping her pen against the desk. "How does someone like Pearce end up dead in a forest, with yet another undeployed parachute? And yet, unlike the others, he was wearing civilian clothing instead of a military uniform. He's not even connected to the war, other than working in a factory that makes parts. Why ever would he be a target?"

"That's the question," Brakes said, rubbing his temples. "And we're no closer to an answer than we were with the first victim." He stood abruptly, pacing the length of the floor. "There has to be a link. These victims are connected somehow, even if we can't see it yet."

Vera watched him thoughtfully, her eyes narrowing. "What if the connection isn't about who they are, but about something they've done? Or something they know?"

Brakes paused mid-stride, considering her words. It was a possibility he hadn't fully explored. The victims may not have had any personal connection to each other, but perhaps they had all been involved in something—whether knowingly or not—that had made them targets.

"I'm going to need to dig deeper into their backgrounds," Brakes said, grabbing his coat from the back of the chair. "Maybe there's something buried in their pasts that we've overlooked."

Nodding, Vera continued working through her own notes while Brakes strode off to try and gather some information on the parachute victims. Addresses of living family members, the last known people they talked to, where they were last seen prior to their grisly deaths... anything that might help him further this investigation and finally put a stop to the murderer. He would have to speak with people of course, interview anyone he could and find out more about these people and any secrets they held. Anything that might point to why they had been targeted, and why they had all met their untimely demise.

As the evening grew later and the sky grew dark, the heaviness of the day weighed down on Brakes. Holding back a yawn, he slowly made his way back to the desk he had been assigned where Vera still sat, now nursing a lukewarm cup of tea.

"Let's call it a night, Vera. We'll find a hotel and try and get some rest. Besides, I could do with a pint." said Brakes tiredly.

"Right, sir; I'll get the car," Vera said, grabbing her hat and briskly making her way out of the station to bring the car round from the back as Brakes waited for her at the side door. Once she stopped in front of him, Brakes jumped in and let out a rather loud yawn.

"Blimey, sir, are you sure you want a pint? It looks like you should go straight to bed." Vera remarked as she drove out of the station.

"Just drive, Vera." Brakes barked, thankful when Vera fell silent and did as she was told. Once they found a hotel, Vera parked the car, and they quickly settled down for a few quiet beers and a bite to eat. Once they were full and sated, they called it a night and headed off to their respective rooms for some much-needed sleep.

When they were making their way back to Norwich the next morning, Brakes could think of nothing but the case; they could finally move forward with the investigation and stitch the pieces together until they finally had a bigger picture. The discovery of this sixth victim had reignited his determination to solve the case, but it also raised more questions than answers.

Brakes knew that uncovering the truth would be difficult. The killer had been meticulous so far, leaving no obvious clues behind. But Brakes also knew that no one could be perfect forever. Sooner or later, the killer would slip up. And when they did, Brakes would be there to catch them.

For now, all he could do was continue to dig, continue to ask questions, and hope that the answers would lead him closer to the truth.

Back at the station, Brakes added the new information to his wall of growing information and evidence on the parachute murders and took a moment to ponder over it once again. He then headed off to the Chief's office to bring him up to date.

That night, as Brakes sat at his kitchen table, staring at the growing collection of the now-copied files and newspaper clippings spread out before him, he couldn't help but feel the weight of the case pressing down on him. The faces of the victims seemed to stare back at him, their unanswered questions haunting his every thought.

He was no closer to understanding the killer's motive, but he knew one thing for certain: judging by the latest victim, the killer wasn't finished yet.

As Brakes drained the last of his tea and set the cup down with a heavy sigh, a knock at the door startled him from his thoughts. He glanced at the clock—it was well past midnight. Who would be visiting at this hour?

He opened the door to find Vera standing there, her face illuminated by the dim light of the hallway.

"I've been thinking," she said, her voice low but insistent. "About what you said earlier. About the connection between the victims."

Brakes raised an eyebrow, intrigued by the look of determination in her eyes.

"I think I might have found something." she said.

Brakes stepped aside, gesturing for her to come in. Whatever Vera had uncovered, it was enough to bring her to his door in the middle of the night. Motioning toward the small kitchen table, which was cluttered with papers, clippings and opened files, Vera crossed the room quickly, her face taut with concentration. Even though she hadn't said much, Brakes knew that look—it was the same look she wore when she was on to something.

"Right," she began, pulling out a small notepad from her pocket as she sat down. "I've been looking into the victims, closer than we have before. You were right; none of them seem to be connected on the surface, but I started thinking about what you said earlier—what if it's not about who they are, but something they've done? Or something they've been involved in, even unknowingly?"

Brakes nodded, leaning forward, hands clasped together as he listened intently. "Go on."

Vera flipped open her notepad and laid it flat on the table. "So, I started digging. I went through old employment records, community files, even hospital admissions—anything that might connect them. And I found something odd."

She paused, tapping her pen against the page. Brakes' eyes narrowed, though he respected Vera's process.

"In the years leading up to their deaths, each one of the victims worked or lived near key military installations. Factories, airbases, munitions depots—places that were heavily involved in the war effort." Vera paused, either for dramatic effect or to simply keep Brakes waiting. She continued. "They didn't have any official connections, but they all spent time in close proximity to these sites."

Brakes straightened in his chair. This was new. "You're saying they were near sensitive military sites? But none of them were military themselves, apart from that mechanic."

"Exactly," Vera said. "But here's the thing: it's not just random. Each victim was in a specific place during a period when security or operations at that site had been compromised in some way—small breaches, usually. Nothing massive, but enough to raise some questions."

Brakes felt a jolt of excitement, though he kept his face controlled. This was exactly the kind of thread he'd been searching for—something that could explain why these ordinary civilians had been killed in such an extraordinary way.

"Give me an example," Brakes said, gesturing for her to continue.

Vera flipped to another page in her notepad. "Alfred Pearce, the sixth victim—the one we just found. He worked in a factory that produced parts for military vehicles, right?"

Brakes nodded. "That's right. Nothing unusual about that."

"Except," Vera said, raising a finger, "that factory had a security breach six months ago. A handful of critical parts went missing from one of the storage depots. It was written off as a theft by black market operators, but no one was ever caught."

Brakes frowned. "So, you think Pearce might have been involved in that? Maybe saw something he wasn't supposed to?"

"It's possible," Vera said. "But it's not just him. Alice Mullins—the nurse, our third victim—worked in a temporary hospital set up near a Royal Air Force base. The base had a similar incident. Some equipment went missing from the hangars, right under the noses of the airmen. Again, no one was ever caught."

Brakes' mind raced as he absorbed the information. If Vera's theory was right, then this wasn't a random pattern of killings. The victims were being targeted because of their proximity to these military installations—possibly because they had witnessed or been unwittingly involved in something bigger.

"So," Brakes said, leaning back in his chair, "you're suggesting that these victims stumbled onto something. Maybe they weren't directly involved, but they were close enough to be a problem for someone."

Vera nodded. "Exactly. But there's more."

Brakes raised an eyebrow. "Go on."

Vera flipped to another page. "I cross-referenced all the victims with records of local police investigations into black market activities. Every one of them lived in areas where black market smuggling operations were taking place. I'm not saying they were part of it, but it's possible they might have seen something or been pressured into silence."

Brakes rubbed his chin thoughtfully. "It's better than what we already have, which is nothing, really. It makes sense." Brakes agreed. The war had created a shadow economy—black market operators, smugglers, and even corrupt officials. It was entirely possible that these victims had crossed paths with dangerous people without even knowing it.

But there was still one detail that bothered him.

"Why the parachutes?" Brakes asked, his brow furrowing. "If this is about covering up black market activities or military thefts, why go through the trouble of staging the bodies like this? Why the uniforms and the parachutes?"

Vera hesitated, clearly thinking through the same question. "I've been trying to figure that out," she admitted. "It's almost theatrical, isn't it? Like someone's sending a message. But who's the message for? Us? The military? Or someone else entirely?"

Brakes stood and walked over to the wall of copied clippings, his eyes scanning the familiar faces of the victims. The parachutes, the military uniforms—those were deliberate choices. It was as if the killer wanted them to see the victims as something they weren't; soldiers, airmen, people involved in the war effort. But the victims weren't soldiers. They were civilians—ordinary people who had inadvertently got caught up in something far beyond their control.

Brakes turned back to Vera. "We need to dig deeper into these black-market connections," he said, his voice firm. "If these victims were silenced because they saw or knew something, then we're dealing with a network that's bigger than just a few isolated thefts. This could be organised and if that's the case, we'll need to find the head of the snake."

Vera nodded, already jotting down notes. "I'll start looking into known operators in the areas where the victims lived. There's bound to be someone who knows more."

Brakes nodded in agreement. "And I'll pay a visit to the military liaison. They will have a full record of these breaches. There might be a connection, or if there's something bigger going on with these installations, they'll know about it."

He paused, already thinking about their next move. After a moment he let out a tired sigh before giving Vera a flippant wave of his hand. "You were right to come over with this, even at this late hour. We'll get to work on these tender lines of enquiry first thing in the morning."

The next morning, Brakes and Vera made their way to the local military liaison office, a small but bustling building near the city centre. The war had strained resources everywhere, but military and civilian cooperation was vital to keeping things running smoothly, especially in a city like Norwich.

Brakes met with Captain Robert Sinclair, a sharp-eyed man in his mid-forties who had a reputation for being both efficient and thorough. Brakes had dealt with him before, though they hadn't always seen eye to eye.

"What brings you here today, Inspector?" Sinclair asked, eyeing Brakes warily as they sat down in his modest office. Vera stood behind him like a statue, her hands clasped behind her back.

Brakes wasted no time. "I need to know if there's any record of military equipment or sensitive materials going missing from installations in Lincolnshire, Suffolk, Norfolk, and Essex over the past four years. Specifically, places near where our six parachute victims lived or worked. Here are the locations."

Pulling out a map and spreading it over the desk, Brakes pointed to the circled locations he and Vera had pin-pointed hours earlier, in preparation for this meeting.

Sinclair's expression hardened. "You think there's a connection between these deaths and military thefts?"

"At this time, we are looking at every angle, but yes, I do," Brakes said. "And I think these people might have been killed because they saw something they weren't supposed to."

Sinclair leaned back in his chair, considering Brakes' words for a moment. "I can tell you that there have been small incidents—missing equipment, minor breaches in security. But nothing that's been flagged as a major threat to national security."

"That's not surprising," Brakes replied. "But I'm not looking for major incidents. I'm looking for a pattern—something that ties these victims to the black-market operators who are smuggling military goods."

Sinclair sighed, running a hand through his greying hair. "I'll see what I can find. But if you're right about this, Inspector, then why has it been missed before? Heads might roll if I do find something."

"That's a problem for you; I have my own issues. Besides, it will be a military police case, so it's out of my jurisdiction. I will wait for your call, Sinclair. Thank you for your time."

Brakes and Vera took their leave and returned to the station. Once they were at his desk, they immediately began going over the possibilities that their newest lead could bring. If they received the information they were hoping for, then it would be like a line of dominoes; when one fell, all of the others would quickly follow.

Whoever was behind these killings was careful—methodical, even. But there was also the possibility that, without realising it, they just might have made a mistake. By targeting people who were close to military installations, they had created a possible pattern. And now Brakes and Vera were following that pattern, which meant that they were one step closer to uncovering the truth.

The hours ticked by and the day soon came to its end. There was nothing from Sinclair by the time the sun went down, so Brakes called it a day and asked Vera to take him home.

The drive there was silent aside from the hum of the engine and the wind that rattled against the car. By the time they arrived at Brakes' cottage, the day had finally given way to the creeping darkness of the night.

Despite living on the edge of the city, Brakes still had to adhere to the blackout conditions stipulated throughout Britain. Closing his curtains first, he then proceeded to switch on the light in his home before removing his coat and hat, which he threw on his favourite armchair.

Making himself a couple of jam sandwiches and a strong cup of tea, Brakes sat down at his kitchen table, his eyes roving over the files that were spread out before him. The information he had gathered over the past day swam around in his mind, unrelenting, and Brakes couldn't shake the feeling that they just might have found the break they were looking for.

Except now Brakes had a sinking feeling that the next victim might already be marked for death. It was just a gut feeling, but one that he couldn't shake.

CHAPTER ELEVEN

The next morning came around far too quickly. Brakes was late up—he had slept through his alarm, something he had never done. Rolling out of bed, he started to get ready in a rush and managed to finish just in time for Vera's arrival. As he was grabbing his coat and hat, he heard the familiar blare of her car horn as she pulled up outside of Brakes' cottage. Slipping his outdoor garments on, Brakes headed out to the car and jumped in, now slightly out of breath.

"To the station, Vera," he panted, earning him an arched brow from his driver as she struck up the engine, and the car burst to life.

"You're looking and sounding a little flustered this morning, sir. Are you okay?" Vera asked.

"I am fine, just late up. I overslept and haven't even had my coffee this morning, so I could be a little grumpy." Brakes replied gruffly.

Vera nodded and thankfully, she did not talk during the drive to the station. She simply drove, allowing Brakes some much needed peace before they finally pulled up. As the car rolled to a stop, Brakes immediately exited the vehicle and strode into the station. His first point of call was the common area, where he would secure his first cup of coffee for the day.

Brakes was only a few feet away from the promise of caffeine—he could practically smell the freshly brewed beans, begging to be sipped—only to be stopped in his tracks by a loud, angry roar bursting from the Chief's office.

"Brakes! Get in here *now!*"

Brakes stopped in his tracks and turned to find the Chief standing outside his door, his face a dangerous red.

"One moment, Chief," he called back, only to hear the anger bubble over in the Chief's next words.

"No, you will come see me right now," the Chief snarled, his tone cold and authoritative. "Get in here, Brakes."

Sighing, Brakes spun on his heel and started walking toward the Chief's office. The promise of coffee grew further from his grasp with each step he took, each thud of his foot hollower than the last. Behind him, he could hear Vera's familiar footfalls as she followed close behind him, but before either of them could enter the Chief's office, their superior zeroed in on them.

"This is nothing to do with you, Constable Stanshore." the Chief snapped, his gaze immediately falling on Vera. "Leave us and continue with your duties."

Vera nodded silently, not questioning his order as she turned away to go and find something else to do. Swallowing hard, Brakes stepped into the office and closed the door behind him as the Chief stalked over to his desk and fell into his chair.

"I have had the police commissioner on the phone for the last bloody hour," the Chief hissed, his neck turning an angry purple as he stared Brakes down. "And I can tell you now, I am not happy with what he has had to say, Brakes."

Brakes stared at the Chief, confused. "I haven't done anything wrong, sir," he said simply, his mind swimming with questions now. "I haven't even put one foot out of line. What exactly is going on, Chief? Why aren't you happy with me?"

"Well, believe or not, it's not you I have an issue with this time." the Chief admitted almost begrudgingly. "And you haven't done anything wrong, but the commissioner is demanding your presence at Scotland Yard regarding the parachute case. Apparently, the media have got hold of the story and are headlining with '*Serial Killer loose in England*'."

Brakes blinked, his eyes growing wide. "That wasn't me, Chief. I have only ever speculated that particular theory to you and Vera."

"Yes, yes, I know," the Chief said, his voice now growing weary. "The commissioner hasn't even mentioned that to me. He just wants you in London to head up a special investigation unit."

Brakes nodded, his expression remaining impassive as he took in the news. No wonder the Chief was furious—he was losing one of his detectives to Scotland Yard, which meant that the Chief would now have to step in and take on the black-market cases. It was not exactly ideal, especially when the Chief hadn't hit the streets in years, so to speak. It also did not help that they were already stretched thin as it was.

The summoning from Scotland Yard itself hadn't been a surprise, and Brakes had been expecting it. He had thought from the moment the sixth body was discovered that this case was spiralling into something much bigger than the local police in Suffolk or Norwich could keep a hold of. The press had gotten wind of it, and now there was a fear, however irrational, that a serial killer might be targeting civilians and staging them as military personnel. For a country at war, already teetering on the edge of exhaustion, this was the last thing anyone needed.

Once the Chief had waved him off, still clearly disgruntled by the news, Brakes returned to his desk where Vera was keeping herself busy. Without mincing his words, Brakes instructed her to get the car and take him back home so that he could pack for London.

"London, sir?" Vera asked, her eyes growing wide. "Why London, if I may ask?"

"Just bring the car round, woman," Brakes muttered, his patience growing thin. "I will explain in a moment."

He stalked out of the station and waited outside for Vera. Once she pulled up in front of him, he immediately jumped in the car and quickly explained that he would be going to Scotland Yard, as per the police commissioner's instruction. The news seemed to surprise Vera, who undoubtedly had a few questions already on her mind, but by the time he had explained the situation, they were already pulling up outside his cottage.

Stepping out of the car, Brakes went to go pack while Vera waited for him, a dozen questions ready to spill from her lips the moment he came back. It only took a few minutes before Brakes returned. Throwing his bag onto the backseat, he instructed Vera to take him to the train station as he slammed the door shut.

"What about me, sir? Am I coming with you?" Vera asked hopefully.

"No, not on this one, Vera. I want you to continue with the theft and black-market case while I am gone, though. Interview the Fire station staff and collect as much information as you can on Derek Johnson and Brian Faulkner. I will ring you in a few days for an update."

"Okay, sir, I am on it; I will not let you down."

Ten minutes later, Vera dropped Brakes off at the train station and Brakes walked onto his platform and awaited the London train. Twenty minutes later, Brakes boarded his train.

The train rattled along the tracks as Brakes sat in a dimly lit carriage, staring out the window. Outside, the English countryside blurred by in shades of green and brown, dotted with the occasional blackened shell of a bombed-out farmhouse. The ever-present tension of war hummed in the air, even out here, far from the front lines. His mind, however, wasn't on the war—not directly. It was on the bodies.

Brakes shifted uncomfortably in his seat, adjusting his overcoat as the train jolted through a curve. His fingers absently brushed over the leather strap of the briefcase resting on his lap. Inside were the files—the only tangible link to the mystery that had consumed him for the last four years. Each victim's life had been carefully catalogued and cross-referenced, but still, the missing piece of the puzzle eluded him.

The train's whistle echoed through the foggy landscape, and Brakes leaned his head back against the seat, closing his eyes. His thoughts drifted to Vera. Leaving her behind to handle the black-market investigation in Norwich had been a tough decision, but she had grown into a capable officer. He trusted her. He hadn't said out loud it, of course—Brakes wasn't one for grand declarations of trust or praise— but he knew she could handle herself.

He imagined her now, poring over records, interrogating suspects, her sharp mind working through the complexities of the case with that quiet, determined energy that had made her such an asset to him. There was something refreshing about Vera's way of thinking. She didn't see the world in the same rigid terms that many of his colleagues did. She was willing to entertain the impossible, the improbable— qualities that had proven invaluable in cases like this one, where nothing made sense on the surface.

The train began to slow as it approached London. The city, even from a distance, had a different energy. The skyline was obscured by a hazy layer of smoke and fog, a combination of the ever-present war industry and the smouldering ruins left by the Luftwaffe's bombing raids. And of course, the ever-present barrage balloons that broke up the skyline over London, the heart of the empire, were scarred but unbowed.

As the train pulled into the station, Brakes gathered his belongings and stood. The platform was bustling with activity—military personnel dressed in their correct coloured uniforms, civilians clutching their ration books, mothers with children clinging to their skirts. Despite the war, the city still moved with a sense of purpose, a grim determination that had become the hallmark of wartime Britain.

Brakes made his way through the crowd, his hat pulled low, and his overcoat collar pulled up against the cold wind that whipped through the station. The streets of London felt different now, quieter somehow. There was less chatter, more urgency in people's steps. The war had changed everything—especially here, in the capital, where the danger felt omnipresent. As he walked toward Scotland Yard, Brakes couldn't help but feel a familiar sense of unease creeping into his bones. The case he had been chasing for years was now under the watchful eye of the nation's most elite law enforcement agency. If he didn't solve it soon, someone else would, and that meant losing control over the one thing that had consumed his life for so long.

The offices of Scotland Yard were swarming with activity when Brakes arrived. The polished stone floors echoed with the sound of hurried footsteps, the air thick with the smell of fresh ink and cigarette smoke. Brakes made his way through the labyrinthine halls, nodding curtly at officers who greeted him in passing. He had been here before, of course, but never under such pressing circumstances.

Chief Commissioner David Carrington sat behind an imposing oak desk in a large office on the top floor. He was a stout man in his mid-fifties, with a reputation for being both no-nonsense and deeply concerned with public perception. As Brakes entered, Carrington motioned for him to sit, his expression unreadable.

"Inspector Brakes," he began, his voice clipped, "I trust your journey from Norwich was uneventful?"

"As uneventful as a wartime train ride can be," Brakes replied, setting his briefcase and bag down on the floor beside him.

Carrington leaned forward, his hands folded on the desk in front of him. "Let's get to it, shall we? We've got six bodies now, and the press is already starting to circle. The last thing we need is a public panic about a killer on the loose. So far, we've managed to keep the details contained, but I can't guarantee that will last much longer."

Brakes nodded, sensing the underlying tension in Carrington's voice. Scotland Yard had its hands full with the war effort, and a series of unexplained civilian deaths wasn't something they had the resources or patience to deal with.

"I understand," Brakes said, "but I'm telling you, Commissioner, this isn't just a case of a deranged killer targeting random civilians. There's a pattern here—a deliberate one."

Carrington raised an eyebrow. "A pattern, you say. From what I've seen, all we've got is a string of unconnected victims in military uniforms and parachutes that weren't deployed."

Brakes opened his briefcase and pulled out the files, spreading them across the desk in a careful arrangement. He pointed to the photos of each victim. Of the six, five of their lifeless bodies were dressed in uniforms that didn't belong to them.

"It's not just the uniforms," Brakes explained. "Each of these victims was found near military installations or factories—places critical to the war effort. They weren't military personnel themselves, but they were close enough to something that mattered. I believe they were killed because they either saw something they shouldn't have or were unwittingly caught up in something bigger.

"As you can see from this picture, all the parachutes had in fact been tampered with, to ensure they wouldn't work. I have also contacted Captain Robert Sinclair at the local military liaison office, who I am hoping will provide me with another angle to attack this from."

Carrington studied the photos, his brow furrowing slightly. "And what is it, exactly, that you think they might have witnessed, Brakes?"

"That's what I'm trying to figure out," Brakes admitted. "But I have been toying with the possibility these deaths are tied to the black-market smuggling operations we've been seeing in Norwich and Suffolk. I can't prove it, but I think these victims weren't random—they were targeted because they were in the wrong place at the wrong time."

Carrington leaned back in his chair, considering this for a moment. "So, you're suggesting that these people were silenced? That they were killed to cover up some kind of smuggling operation?"

"Something like that, but it's just speculation at this point." Brakes said. "But it's more than just smuggling. Someone is going to great lengths to make these deaths look like accidents—parachute failures, to be precise. And they're using military uniforms to throw us off the trail, to make it seem like these victims were involved in the war effort when, in fact, they weren't."

Carrington exhaled slowly, his fingers tapping lightly on the desk. "It's a compelling theory, Inspector, but without concrete evidence, I can't authorise any further resources. We're stretched thin as it is, and I can't divert manpower away from more immediate threats to national security."

Brakes clenched his jaw, frustration bubbling up inside him. He had expected this. Scotland Yard wasn't going to allocate resources to a case that wasn't directly tied to the war, but he wasn't about to give up.

"I understand, Commissioner," Brakes said, trying to keep his voice steady. "But I'm asking for your cooperation—let me pursue this case on my own terms. I've already got leads in Suffolk and Norwich, and I believe I'm closing in on finding out why these people died, which will then hopefully lead to who committed these deaths."

Carrington looked at him for a long moment, weighing his options. Finally, he nodded.

"Alright, Brakes. I'll give you some leeway on this. See the duty sergeant downstairs and he will give you an office. I want you to stay here for a few days so that you can keep me directly informed." Carrington explained, his gaze stern. "I want to know every step. But you need to understand—if this goes wrong, if the press gets wind of it and it turns into a circus, you'll be the one answering for it. Do you understand?"

"I understand," Brakes said, standing up and gathering his files.

Carrington leaned forward, his eyes narrowing slightly. "And one more thing, Inspector; if you're right about this, if there really is something bigger going on, then you're dealing with people who won't hesitate to kill again to protect their operation. Be careful."

Brakes nodded, already halfway out the door. He knew the risks. He had known them since the first body was found. But now, with Scotland Yard's reluctant approval, he had the freedom to dig deeper—and he intended to use it.

Brakes headed down to find the duty sergeant and sort an office out. Once settled in, instead of ringing Captain Robert Sinclair at the Norwich military liaison office, he decided to visit their headquarters, which wasn't too far away from the Yard.

Brakes navigated the streets littered with temporary barbwire fences and sandbag-covered buildings with sentries patrolling every entrance checking ID cards. As he walked, he couldn't believe how many of the buildings had bomb damage, much of it minor but the odd one with gaping holes or completely blown out walls.

Once he arrived at the HQ, Brakes headed for the reception. Showing his ID, he requested an audience with someone from the archives. The receptionist swiftly directed him down a short hall until he came across an office marked by a small sign stuck to the wall that said '*Archives*'.

Brakes opened the door and was met with an earthy, woody aroma that hung in the air. Thousands of new and vintage paperwork was stored before him, practically bulging on the shelves that towered behind a rather aged, small statured fellow who was wearing a pair of round spectacles. Stepping into the room, Brakes immediately produced his identity card and introduced himself.

"How may I help you today, Inspector?" asked the man.

"You have had a request from a Captain Robert Sinclair at the Norwich military liaison office, yes?" enquired Brakes.

"I have, sir. It's right here and waiting to be sent off. In fact, I'm waiting for the courier to pick it up." the man replied.

"Would you please ring the Captain. Explain that I am stood in front of you requesting to collect the information in person and asking for his permission to hand it over to me." Brakes asked. Without hesitation, the man picked up the receiver on his desk and began dialling the number for the Norwich military liaison office. Almost immediately the man began speaking into the phone, his voice low, and after a brief conversation he handed the phone over to Brakes.

"Brakes? Brakes, are you there?" asked the voice on the phone.

"Brakes here. Is that you, Sinclair?"

"Yes. Now, listen Brakes, this is highly irregular, as you know. There is a procedure to follow." Sinclair said, a hint of disappointment clear in his voice.

"I fully understand, Sinclair. I am sorry, but things have taken a somewhat hurried turn." Brakes explained. "I have been summoned to Scotland Yard— the Commissioner needs this dealing with post haste. Top priority, you see. So, I need the files now whilst I am in London."

With a reluctant sigh, Sinclair's voice came through the receiver. "Pass me back to the archivist," he requested.

Passing the telephone back to the man, another short conversation passed between Sinclair and the archivist. Finally, the man put the receiver down and with a disdained look on his face, pulled out a form and asked Brakes to sign it. Once Brakes had scribbled his name on the line, the man took out an official stamp and placed it over Brakes' signature before handing over the files that would now aid Brakes in his case.

Thanking the gentleman for his cooperation, Brakes headed out of the archives and into the streets of London. There was a building close by the Yard that was used by all the visiting officers for overnight stays, blackout curtains covering every window. The absence of streetlights made London seem darker than usual, an eerie, almost ghostly quality settling on the once vibrant city. Returning to his digs for the remainder of the evening, Brakes tried to drown out the distant rumble of anti-aircraft fire that echoed across the rooftops, a grim reminder of the constant threat of bombing raides.

CHAPTER TWELVE

Brakes spent most of the evening going over the files from the military archives. He searched tirelessly for any kind of pattern, no matter how miniscule. He just needed something to take back to the Commissioner.

After another dead end in his search, Brakes put the files down and rubbed his eyes. Deciding to take a moment for himself, Brakes stood up to stretch, momentarily relieving the ache that had formed in his back. Letting out a yawn, his thoughts soon drifted back to Vera and decided that he should ring and update her.

It was still early enough that she wouldn't be in bed, so he decided to call her at home. Dialling her number, Brakes continued to twist and turn on the spot whilst the phone rang out, the sound hollow in his ear.

"Norwich 3826, Stanshore speaking." Came the curt, professional reply.

"Vera, it's Brakes. Sorry for the lateness of the call and to bother you at home."

"It's no bother, sir. How is it all going down there?" enquired Vera.

Brakes let out a heavy sigh. "Slow. Too slow, actually. I could do with your sharp eyes with these files. I am still searching for a modus operandi with little to no success." Brakes paused, his mind turning to other matters at hand. "Forgetting that just for a moment, Vera; how are things going with the black-market case?"

"I have taken statements from all the firemen that were on duty that night. All of them were very helpful and forthcoming, to be honest. I don't believe any of them are involved in anything shady, sir." Vera replied.

"Okay. Have you visited the two main players yet?"

"No, sir. I will be doing that tomorrow first thing. I have to say, it's rather strange you not being around. Any idea when you will return, sir?"

"No idea, Vera. The Commissioner wants to keep me down here so that he gets first hand updates. Annoying, I know, but nothing I can do about it." Brakes murmured tiredly, his hand rising to rub at his temples.

"So, you haven't found any patterns or missing itinerary of any kind? Nothing caught your eye?" Vera asked, a hint of disappointment clear in her voice.

Swaying gently on the spot, Brakes' gaze turned to the ceiling. "Well, yes. Items are missing from all locations, but not in large quantities. Nothing I would consider killing for." he explained, his lips curling into a frown. "I am currently looking at delivery personnel, but again, it's a dead end. Each unit has different drivers due to their different locations around the country."

"What about the pilots, sir?"

"That is my next avenue of enquiry, as a matter of fact." Brakes replied, and he was almost certain he could hear Vera nod on the other end of the phone.

"Okay, sir." Vera answered. There was a short pause before her voice returned. "Well, if there is nothing else, I will bid you good evening." And then she put the receiver down, silence quickly filling the air of Brakes' room.

Turning back to his desk, Brakes returned to the dismal task of looking through the files to find something, *anything,* that would produce results. Turning his attention to the files on all the registered pilots at all the nearby bases, Brakes combed through the information. Yet, despite his search, he could not name one that had transferred or even visited all the bases at the time of the undeployed parachute deaths.

By the time the clock was ticking closer to midnight, Brakes' eyes had grown heavy with tiredness, and he knew that it was time to finish up for the night. Putting down the papers, Brakes got ready for bed and quickly fell asleep.

Around the hour of 02:40, Brakes awoke with a jolt and bolted upright in his bed. Sweat dripped all over his body, his pyjamas now soaked through. Throwing the damp covers off of him, he took off his shirt and started to wipe himself down with it, his breath heavy and ragged with each swipe. Once he was sufficiently dryer than he had been, Brakes stood and walked over to the water jug and bowl to rinse himself off.

As he took a moment to catch his breath, Brakes recalled what had awoken him. Not a dream, but in fact a heart-stopping nightmare.

He had been falling through the sky, just as the victims had. His eyes had been wide-open, his mind fused in fear, and he could see the ground below him, inching closer and closer.

And there was nothing he could do about it.

His body had been falling at breakneck speed, his throat raw as each scream was swallowed up by the bright blue sky. Then, just as he was certain he would touch the ground, each bone breaking upon impact, Brakes had woken up.

Taking a deep, fortifying lungful of air at the horrifying memory of his nightmare, Brakes finished cleaning himself up and threw on a clean pyjama top. Making himself a much-needed mug of tea, he sat on the edge of his bed for a while and tried to think of anything but the case. If he was going to get anymore sleep, he first needed to clear his mind.

Picking up yesterday's paper, he decided to have a go at the crossword. After a half hour or so, Brakes had finished his tea and solved a few of the answers before finally deciding to switch off the light once more and lay his head down for another attempt at sleep.

Brakes managed to get a few more hours of sleep before he awoke again. It was just after the dawn had broken, and he immediately got out of bed to start his day.

After polishing off his breakfast of toast and scrambled eggs, Brakes began stripping down his bed and picked up the sweat-soaked pyjama top before taking them downstairs. There, he found the buildings warden and asked if they could wash them for him, which they gladly obliged.

Making his way back down the hallway, Brakes knew that it was too early for him to head for the yard but decided that it was best to get an early start on the day, so headed off to the station, anyway.

Scotland Yard loomed ahead, a fortress of authority nestled within the ever-bustling heart of London. Brakes stood outside for a moment, letting the brisk wind tug at the edges of his overcoat. Even as a seasoned detective, the sight of the Yard was enough to remind him of the gravity of the task ahead. This was where cases came to be solved, or where they disappeared into bureaucratic labyrinths, never to be seen again. The pressure was palpable, and Brakes felt it settling in his chest as he crossed the threshold into the imposing stone building.

The interior of the Yard was as cold and unyielding as the exterior. Polished marble floors, high ceilings, and the constant echo of footfalls created an atmosphere both official and impersonal. It was a place that radiated with the weight of justice.

As he made his way down the corridor, Brakes could feel eyes on him. Officers nodded in his direction, either in acknowledgment or curiosity. Everyone knew he had been called to London about the parachute deaths. It wasn't every day that a local shire detective was summoned to Scotland Yard, and the whispers were already making their way through the ranks.

The case had taken on a life of its own, especially after the discovery of the sixth victim. People were beginning to wonder if the police were dealing with something more than just a series of strange accidents. The fear of a killer on the loose, hiding under the guise of war, was starting to creep into the public consciousness.

Opening his office door, Brakes flicked on the light and slapped the files he had received from Sinclair down on his desk. Pulling out the chair, Brakes sat down and immediately began tapping his fingertips on top the closed file.

Finally, after a moment of pondering, Brakes flipped open the file and started sifting through each page once more. Then he turned back to the pilot lists, his eyes raking over the words.

"It has to be a pilot," he thought to himself with a frown. *"But clearly it wasn't any one of the enlisted ones. So, who else would fly a plane?"*

After a long moment, Brakes' gaze caught something, and his eyes grew wide.

"Got it!" he cried out to the empty room. "I finally figured it out. It simply can't be anyone else; someone from the ATA has to be the killer!"

The ATA—the Airport Transport Auxiliary— were a civilian organisation that worked alongside the enlisted men and women. Their job included delivering new, repaired and damaged military aircraft's to and from factories and maintenance units, as well as to active squadrons around the country. Aside from the pilots, it was the ATA who also had the means and the opportunity to stage such deaths.

Gathering up his papers, Brakes knew it was time to bring the Commissioner up to date. He would need to try and talk him into bringing more people onto the case, too—the ATA had hundreds of personnel scattered all over the country, and Brakes would need more than himself to look further into this case.

Brakes headed for the Commissioner's office. Once he was standing outside of the door, he took a momentary pause to collect himself. Carrington had always been a no-nonsense leader, a man whose reputation had been built on solving high-profile cases. But wartime had changed him, as it had changed so many others. The pressure of maintaining order during the chaos of bombings, rationing, and civilian unrest had left its mark, making him more cautious and more driven to protect the Yard's reputation. If this case wasn't solved quickly, Brakes knew that Carrington would find someone else to blame, and that person would be him.

Brakes knocked once and stepped inside.

The office was dimly lit, despite the daylight streaming through the window. The heavy curtains kept much of the sunlight at bay, casting long shadows across the room. Carrington sat behind a large, cluttered desk, his brow furrowed in thought. The man's demeanour from the day before had been replaced by an air of impatience and frustration. He didn't waste time with pleasantries.

"What can I do for you, Brakes?" Carrington asked without looking up. His voice was low but sharp, each word cutting through the silence. Before Brakes could reply, Carrington continued. "Let me remind you, this case needs to be solved, and it needs to be solved quickly. The newspapers are already stirring up trouble, questioning why the police haven't made more progress. We've managed to keep the details of the parachute deaths from causing a full-blown panic, but that won't last if we don't get results."

Brakes nodded grimly. Standing just inside the door, he clutched his hat in one hand. "I realise as much, **Commissioner**. It's only a matter of time before the press gets wind of the connections between the victims. Once they do, they'll run wild with it."

Carrington glanced up at him, his eyes narrowing. "Exactly. And we can't afford that kind of distraction right now, not with the war effort stretched thin and people already on edge. You've seen the headlines—families torn apart by bombings, food shortages, black-market dealings. Now add a potential serial killer into the mix, and the public will lose faith in us."

Brakes remained silent for a moment, letting Carrington's words sink in. The pressure was immense, and he knew the consequences if they failed to make progress soon. But what bothered him most was the feeling that the case was on the verge of unravelling.

"I've reviewed the file I got from the military liaison office last night once again this morning, and I think I now have a solid lead on the killer, sir." Brakes said carefully, stepping forward to place the file on the desk. "This is my theory which emerged this morning—an unsettling possibility that we haven't considered before."

Carrington raised an eyebrow, motioning for him to continue.

"I have found a connection between the locations where the bodies have been found and nearby airfields or factories, all critical to the war effort. But one particular detail stood out—the involvement of the ATA, the Air Transport Auxiliary," Brakes said, pulling out several documents and photos. "Specifically, and most certainly, it has to be one of the female pilots from the ATA. I say female, because they are mainly all women."

Carrington's expression darkened. "A female pilot?"

Brakes nodded. "It's speculation for now; we need to link the deaths to the presence of ATA flights in that area first, then we can narrow down the suspects by checking the logs. The parachutes, the uniforms—it's all too specific. And the ATA, as you know, isn't bound by the same strict protocols as the RAF. They're civilians, flying military aircraft from one base to another, often with little oversight."

Carrington leaned back in his chair, rubbing his temples. "If this is true—if there's someone within the ATA using their position to commit these murders—it could be disastrous. The ATA is essential to the war effort. The government would bury this story in an instant if they thought it would in any way damage morale or trust in the war machine."

Brakes sighed. "I know. That's why we need to tread carefully. But there's something else that's been bothering me about this case, and that's the precision of it all. These aren't simple crimes of passion; they're calculated, methodical." Brakes explained, his voice falling low as Carrington listened intently. "The victims weren't random. Someone has been targeting them for a reason, and the way the bodies were left, with unopened parachutes in military uniforms, suggests an intimate knowledge of aviation and the military system. It's almost like a message is being sent."

Carrington stared at him for a long moment, the gears turning in his head. "So, we need to narrow down a specific suspects list?"

"Yes, sir." Brakes admitted. "But I'm working on it. I have started looking into all ATA personnel who had access to the areas where the victims were found. If we can narrow it down, we might be able to find a pattern, or a motive."

Carrington stood up, walking over to the window and staring out at the city below. The distant wail of sirens and aircraft engines could be heard.

"You realise how dangerous this could get, don't you? If someone within the ATA is involved, we're dealing with a person who has access to military aircraft's, sensitive information, and the ability to move across the country without raising suspicion."

Brakes nodded. "I understand. But we can't back down now. If we don't stop this person, there will be more bodies. I just hope that the next one will be the one where they make a mistake."

Carrington turned back to face Brakes, his expression grim. "Alright, Brakes. You have my permission to continue investigating this angle. I will assemble some other trustworthy personnel to help you but keep it quiet; the last thing we need is for this to leak before we have solid evidence. If the press gets wind of it, we'll have a full-blown scandal on our hands."

"I'll be discreet." Brakes assured him.

Carrington walked back to his desk and sat down heavily, rubbing his chin in thought. "And what about the black-market investigation in Norwich? Any leads there?"

Brakes hesitated for a moment before answering. "I've left that in the hands of my driver, Vera. She's been helping me with the case, and I trust her to handle it. She's resourceful."

Carrington raised an eyebrow, a faint hint of scepticism in his expression. "Your driver? Hasn't she has only just completed the police training, Brakes? I hope you know what you're doing."

"She's not just a driver, sir. Vera's officially a sworn-in officer now, and she's proven herself to be more than capable." Brakes replied firmly. "She has a way of seeing things from a different perspective, and I think she might be able to dig up something that the rest of us have missed."

Carrington nodded slowly. "Alright. But make sure you stay on top of both investigations. We can't afford to lose focus."

Nodding, Brakes gathered his files and turned to leave, but Carrington's voice stopped him at the door.

"Brakes," he called, his tone softer yet somehow more intense. "Be careful. Whoever's behind this, there is no doubt they're dangerous. And they're not going to stop until they've finished whatever they've set out to do."

Brakes met his gaze, a silent understanding passing between them. "I know," he said quietly. "But neither am I."

Turning back to his paperwork, Carrington waved a dismissive hand. "Head for the briefing room, Brakes. Third floor. By the time you arrive, your team should already be waiting."

CHAPTER THIRTEEN

Gathering the Team

Brakes left the Chief Commissioner's office with a renewed sense of purpose but also a growing sense of urgency. Carrington's words echoed in his mind: *Keep it quiet.* It was easier said than done when the bodies were piling up, and with the press sniffing around like hungry wolves.

Stopping outside of the briefing room, Brakes paused for a moment, gathering his thoughts. He was about to walk into a room full of strangers—his new team. London officers with their own methods, their own habits. But he couldn't afford to waste time worrying about fitting in. This case required results, and that meant getting everyone on the same page, and quickly.

Pushing open the door, Brakes entered the briefing room where he was introduced to the team that would be assisting him. There were four of them—three detectives and a forensic analyst, all seasoned officers who had seen their share of wartime chaos.

At the head of the table sat Detective Sergeant William Ford, the most senior of the group and a grizzled veteran with a reputation for being as tough as they come. Next to him was Detective Constable Helen Marks, a sharp-eyed woman in her early thirties who had a knack for connecting seemingly unrelated details. Then there was Constable Michael Parry, fresh-faced but eager to prove himself, and finally, there was Dr. Albert Shaw, a forensic expert who had been dealing with everything from bomb victims to murder victims since the Blitz began.

Wasting no time, Brakes set his briefcase on the table and nodded to the team.

"Good afternoon, everyone. I'm Detective Inspector Brakes, from Norwich. The Chief Commissioner has put us together in an effort to solving and apprehending the perpetrator of these grisly parachute murders." he began, his voice loud and clear as everyone turned to him. "Now, this parachute case has caught the attention of the higher-ups, and we're going to find out who's behind them."

He could feel their eyes on him, weighing his words. These weren't just new faces—they were his colleagues now; the people he'd be relying on to help him solve this case.

"We've got six bodies over the course of three years, five found in military uniforms. The latest victim was dressed in civilian clothes, however. All parachutes were undeployed." Peering at each member of the team, Brakes' mouth twisted into a grim frown. He continued. "The media's caught wind of the latest one in Suffolk, and the public's starting to ask questions. This case isn't going to stay quiet much longer, and we need to move fast, before the killer strikes again."

Ford leaned back in his chair, crossing his arms. "You think they're connected?"

Brakes nodded. "I do. Each victim was staged,dDressed in military uniforms, found with parachutes, but none of them had any training that would suggest they were in the service, except one. Whoever is doing this knows what they're doing, and they've managed to cover their tracks well enough that these deaths were initially ruled as accidents."

Marks tapped a pen on the table, her brow furrowed. "Do we have any leads?"

"The only things we know for sure is, firstly, the parachutes were tampered with, all in the same way, as you can see here," Brakes said, picking the parachute up and showing the officers where they had been sewn up. "Secondly, I have narrowed the suspect list to it being someone from the ATA. I've talked to families, friends, employers, but none of the victims had any connection to each other. That's the strange part. It feels random, but the execution is too specific to be the work of an amateur."

Dr. Shaw, the forensic expert, cleared his throat. "I've reviewed the initial reports. From what I can tell, the injuries were consistent with falling from a great height—exactly what you'd expect if the parachutes failed to open. But if we can get a closer look at one of the bodies, we might find something the previous investigators missed."

Brakes frowned; he knew that exhuming bodies would be a delicate matter. He had already considered it but needed something more concrete to justify such an action. The fact that Shaw was on board gave him a glimmer of hope.

"Let's come back to that later, Doctor. Here are all the case files," Brakes said, pulling out the case files and laying them on the table. "We'll need to comb through each victim's background again. We're missing something—a link, a clue. And we'll need to look into the parachutes themselves. Who could have supplied them? Were they stolen, purchased, or repurposed?"

Ford leaned forward. "We'll also need to check military records. Someone had to have access to those uniforms. Either they're fakes, or our killer has connections."

"Agreed," Brakes said. "I've already requested military records from the local bases, but it'll take time. For now, we work with what we've got. Finally, we need to put together a list of possible killers. Check and cross reference all the active ATA personnel against the dates each victim was found and see if anyone was in that area at the same time."

There was a hum of chatter as Brakes' new team got to work, intrigue already spiking the air. Over the course of the next few hours, each person pored over the details of each victim, tracing their steps, and trying to find any connection between them. The atmosphere in the room was tense but focused, and each officer brought their expertise to the table. Slowly, they began to piece together a clearer picture.

Ford was methodical, reviewing the logistics of each discovery site, analysing travel routes, and looking into any nearby military facilities. Marks was quick to pick up on inconsistencies in witness statements and family interviews, while Parry combed through old police reports, searching for any mention of military equipment thefts or unexplained parachute drops.

By the time meeting came to its end, Brakes felt something akin to relief as he watched his new team filter out. For the first time in years, he wasn't working alone, and the familiar thrill of the hunt was beginning to course through him once again. The collective minds of his team were bringing fresh perspectives, and he could feel the momentum building. But he knew they were still far from the answers they needed.

He would need to work fast, though. The war had made everything more complicated, and time was not on their side. As Brakes packed his files away, his mind turned to Vera, still working on the black-market case back in Norwich. She had her own battle to fight, but in that moment, Brakes admitted to himself that he missed having her by his side.

It was undeniable that the dynamic between them had changed in the time they had known each other, and Brakes found himself thinking about her more often than he cared to admit. Shaking off the thought, Brakes picked up his briefcase and headed for the door. There was no time for distractions, not now.

Stepping out into the crisp London evening, the sound of distant explosions rumbled in the air. Standing outside of Scotland Yard, Brakes took a deep breath and allowed the cool air to settle his thoughts.

The weight of responsibility from his meeting with the Chief Commissioner still hung heavily on his shoulders. Scotland Yard was now involved, and with a full team at his disposal, there was no turning back.

Pulling his coat tighter around him, Brakes made his way back toward his digs, ready for an early night. He needed sleep—this was not the time to be running on empty batteries.

Looking up at the sky while bombs set off in the distance, Brakes was hopeful that he might finally get some answers. He had a team behind him now, and as sure as the war raged on, so did Brakes.

And he wouldn't stop until he had brought the killer to justice.

CHAPTER FOURTEEN

The next morning, Brakes woke early. He headed straight to the Yard and shut himself in his office. By the time the rest of the team arrived, Brakes was already making a list of potential suspects.

The room quickly became a mess of activity with everyone else's input, and before long, the suspect list was already growing into the double figures.

At some point during their discussion, Ford had left the room to go down to the archives. Once he returned, he came back with the news that he had found a possible unsolved break-in at a military depot back in 1937, up in Cumbria. Adding the newly found information to the chalkboard, he circled the information with the words, '*Follow up*' beside it.

Once the board was sufficiently filled, Brakes told the team that he would be taking an hour for himself. Throwing on his coat and hat, Brakes walked the streets of London in an effort to clear his mind.

For four years this cast had consumed his mind and gnawed at his soul. It had taken its toll on him in many ways—a gruesome, baffling enigma that had slowly been devouring him the more time went on. And now he had finally caught a thread, a frayed end poking out of the tangled mess.

The ATA was the new link between the murders and with a new team behind him, still hard at work narrowing down a list of suspects, Brakes knew that they were on the verge of cracking open this mystifying case.

Making his way back, Brakes pushed open the heavy oak door of Scotland Yard. The familiar scent of dust and stale tobacco clung to the air, his footsteps echoing off the walls as he made his way back to the office. He was immediately met with the sight of his team, their own faces etched with the same weariness he felt as they sat together, cramped and bumping shoulders every time they moved.

"Right," Brakes barked, their attention quickly turning to him. "Sorry about that; I needed to clear my head. How are we doing on the ATA pilot list, people?"

"It's going to be another couple of days until we complete the list," Helen Marks replied with a frown. "As you know, there are hundreds of them."

Brakes nodded, aware that this task would take time they did not have. But his team were trying their best and, while he wished they could work faster, he appreciated how far they had already come along with the case.

"I did notice something though, sir," Marks added, breaking Brakes away from his thoughts. "I was going through the victim's files again, just to keep it fresh in my mind, you know. Anyway, something jumped out at me—Peter Hall, the first victim—I noticed in his personal possessions list, he was wearing a pair of US military socks."

"And?" Brakes asked, his gaze fixed squarely on Marks. Pressing his lips together, he waited for her to continue.

"Well, it's like this, sir; the Special Branch have been investigating a murder case with twelve victims, all of whom were found wearing US military issue socks," she explained. Brakes raised his eyebrows, his curiosity undeniably piqued by this new piece of information. Marks continued. "I think you should go down and have a word with Inspector Davies. It might just be a coincidence but, nevertheless, it's worth a chat, hey?"

Nodding in agreement, Brakes headed toward his desk and sat himself down. "Right; I will finish this pile of files on the ATA personnel and then nip down to see him." he replied, already reaching for the aforementioned files.

"Just ask him about the 'sock murder' case, sir." Marks replied, her gaze shifting back to her own work as silence settled on the room.

A little later on, Brakes was slumped in his chair and nursing a cup of lukewarm tea. With a stifled yawn, he finished off the pile of files on his desk and stood up to add any newly found names to the office list that now lined the blackboard. Finally, he began rereading the file on Peter Hall.

It wasn't that he had overlooked Hall's socks—it was simply a case of Brakes not knowing that there had been other murders, especially the kind that were linked to military issue socks. Flipping back to the personal effects page of Peter Halls' file, Brakes scanned over the words that had been listed there. A packet of fags, a ration book…

Brakes' breath hitched as he read over the next line of words.

"US Army issue socks," he muttered to himself, reading over the line again. Marks had been right.

Surging to his feet, Brakes knocked over his teacup in his haste to leave the room and hardly noticed the lukewarm liquid spread across his desk and the files he had abandoned.

Marching down the corridor, Brakes' gut churned with a mixture of dread and grim anticipation. If these cases were somehow connected, then there was a chance that the parachute murders were far bigger than anyone could have anticipated.

Finding himself at the Special Branches door, Brakes knocked briskly before entering. He knew the head by sight; Inspector Davies, a taciturn man with eyes that had seen too much.

Davies' office was a fortress of files and locked cabinets. He looked up, his expression unreadable. "Brakes. To what do I owe the pleasure?"

"I need to see the files on the 'Sock Murders'," Brakes said, his voice tight. Davies' eyebrows rose slightly.

"That old chestnut? Those files are sealed, Brakes. Classified. No connection to your… parachute business, I assure you." Davies said, a hint of disbelief in his voice.

"I found US Army issue socks on my first victim, Peter Hall. That's enough of a connection for me." Replied Brakes, his tone quickly becoming urgent.

Davies stared at him for a long moment, his face impassive. Then, with a sigh that seemed to carry the weight of the world, he unlocked a heavy steel cabinet.

"Six years, Brakes," he said, pulling out a thick file bound in faded canvas. "Twelve victims. Men and women. All murdered in different ways. Stabbings, poisonings, drownings... no pattern. No discernible motive. The only thing they had in common was a pair of US Army issue socks worn by each victim."

Taking the files from Davies, Brakes leafed through the grim documentation. For each victim there was a photograph plastered brutally to the page, each death a grotesque tableau of violence. He felt a cold dread creeping through him, a sense of vast, unfathomable evil.

He stopped at the photograph of Elizabeth Croft, a librarian found drowned in Hyde Park six years prior. Her pale face, staring blankly from the page, held a chilling familiarity.

"Elizabeth Croft," Davies said, following his gaze. "First victim. We thought the socks were a red herring, a coincidence. But then they kept appearing, and the victims kept piling up."

Brakes closed the file, the weight of it heavy in his hands.

"Elsie Cartwright, the second victim, worked at the military supply factory. She would have had access to supplies still held there from WWI, meant for the American forces, including a ready supply of socks. She was also in London, a possible link to several of the sock murders." Davies recalled.

A terrifying picture was beginning to form in Brakes' mind. A picture of a meticulously planned and ruthlessly executed series of murders, stretching back six years, connected by a single, chilling thread: US Army issue socks.

"Special Branch has been looking for a pattern," Davies said, his voice low. "A method. A motive. We've found nothing. Maybe you finding one of your victims wearing those socks means you've found a connection between your case and this one?"

Brakes' mind raced. The ATA, the military supply factory, the US Army socks... the pieces were starting to fall into place. It was as if the parachute murders and the sock murders were not a separate, unrelated crime. They were simply different facets of the same terrible darkness. At least, that's what both Davies and Brakes were now thinking.

Brakes looked at Davies, his eyes filled with a grim determination. "We need to work together, Davies. This isn't just about parachutes or socks anymore—this is about a killer operating in the shadows, weaving a web of death. And we need to stop them. We had best go and speak to the commissioner about our findings, see if he agrees to a merging of the cases.”

The two of them immediately made their way to the commissioner's office and brought him up to date. Thankfully, once they had explained their findings, the commissioner needed little convincing on the matter.

“This is now a nationwide manhunt; I will inform all stations to provide you with anything you require.” The commissioner said, his palms planted firmly on his desk as he peered at Brakes and Davies through dark, stormy eyes. “Now, stop wasting time hovering. Get out of here and catch this man or woman!”

Standing tall, the commissioner pointed at his office door, his face turning a dangerous shade of red as Brakes and Davies each gave a quick nod before scurrying out of the office and into the corridor.

As Davies and Brakes made their way back to their respective offices, they knew that this alliance would be uneasy. Both investigations had been separated by years of frustration and unsolved mystery, and now they had somehow converged, all thanks to military issue socks.

CHAPTER FIFTEEN

When Brakes returned to his office, he could see that the team were still hard at work. DC Marks had continued to check on Peter Hall's file, searching for anything that might further the case. He was currently the only victim that seemingly had no family—to their knowledge, there were no contact details or even interviews with family members in his file.

"Parry, can you visit the archives for me? I need you to check the local records for Eden, Cumbria, and find out the dates and place of Hall's parents' deaths." Marks asked the youngest of their team. Parry straightened to attention immediately.

"You hoping to find something, Detective Constable?" Parry asked curiously, focusing on Marks.

"Just need to confirm their places and dates of death. And while you have them on the phone, check their cause of death too, just to be thorough." Marks confirmed, barely looking up from Hall's file. With a final nod, Parry exited the office to do as he was asked and passed Brakes on his way out.

Making his way back to the desk, Brakes had barely sat in his seat when Ford strolled up to him, his eyebrows pinched together.

"Ford," Brakes said politely. Thankfully, the sergeant didn't waste any time with pleasantries and went straight to the point.

"I have found a military depot that has been involved in several break-ins over the past few years," he revealed, causing Brakes to sit up straight with interest. "Interestingly, it is located in Cumbria."

Brakes' eyebrows shot up, his eyes wide. "Is there anything else?" he asked. Ford simply shook his head.

"I have looked over the file thoroughly, but it only provides the time and dates of the robberies. There are no confirmed suspects." he explained. Brakes sighed, though he was not entirely disappointed; this was another step in the right direction, another lead that could help them to find the murderer and solve this cold case.

"Then it requires further investigation," Brakes replied. "I think that it is best for me to stay here and oversee the case. I will dispatch you to Cumbria. Look into the robberies a little more closely and if there is anything, anything you can find, report it to us the moment you return. Do you hear me?"

"Understood, sir." Ford said and without another word, turned on his heel and returned to his work while Brakes made the necessary calls for Ford's imminent dispatch to Cumbria.

Ford returned a few days later, his face grim. "The depot owner remembers the incidents like they were yesterday," he said. "A large number of socks went missing, along with some other supplies on every occasion. They suspected it was an inside job, but they never caught anyone."

"Did they have any suspects?" Brakes asked.

Ford hesitated. "They had one. An airman named John Smith. He was transferred shortly after the incident. No formal charges were ever filed, but the owner said he wouldn't be surprised if Smith was involved."

John Smith. The name rang a bell. Leaning over his desk, Brakes began rifling through the ATA personnel files and there it was: John Smith. A British pilot, recruited from America. Brakes' heart pounded. Could it be? An American airman, suspected of stealing socks, who later became an ATA pilot. It was too much of a coincidence.

"Marks, pull up Smith's flight logs," Brakes barked, and Marks immediately did as she was told. Once she had retrieved the needed logs, Brakes flipped through them, scanning each log quickly and efficiently. They were extensive, covering flights all over the country. Brakes compared the dates and locations of Smith's flights to the dates and locations of the parachute murders and the 'Sock Murders'. A chilling pattern quickly emerged:

Smith had been in the vicinity of every single murder.

"Marks," Brakes said, his voice tight. "Get me everything you can find on John Smith. I want his background, his contacts, family, everything."

As Marks raced to comply, Brakes picked up the phone and called a contact he had made at a local radar station in Suffolk. "I need you to do something for me," he said, his voice low. "I need you to track any single aircraft, particularly those with no IFF signal. It's likely a light aircraft, possibly a Tiger Moth... Well, just any aircraft. I don't want you to shoot it down, but I want you to keep an eye on it. Report its movements to me immediately if you come across anything, that is."

He repeated the same request to radar stations across the country, his network of contacts clicking into gear. He had a feeling Smith might just be the killer they were searching for.

Just as Brakes put the phone down, Parry raced into the office clutching several pieces of paper.

"Sir, ma'am, I finally have the details you requested a few days ago," Parry said, his face red and chest heaving as he blurted out his findings. "As you can see, Hall's mother died in hospital in 1933. But there is no record regarding his father. He seems to have vanished completely."

Handing over the papers, Parry stepped back as Brakes and Marks scanned over this newfound evidence, another piece to help complete their ever-growing puzzle of mysteries.

"So, the father cannot be found anywhere?" Asked Brakes.

"If you look at page four, sir, you will see his military record from World War One. Fred Hall, his father, was a decorated corporal and pilot of WWI. Aged in his late 40's. He volunteered for service on the outset of WWII as a pilot but washed out after basic flight training due to his broken mind set." Parry explained, watching as Brakes and Marks continued to look over the files he had obtained for them.

"Hm, yes, I can see that," Brakes muttered, finding the information Parry had just verbalised on the paper. "It says 'war neurosis', though we more commonly refer to it as 'Shell Shock'."

"But there's nothing after that," Marks added with a frown, her own sharp eyes scanning over the last page. "He seems to have simply fallen off the face of the earth."

"People, we may have just found our second suspect." Brakes announced to the room. There was a deafening silence just moments before everyone erupted into chatter, a thrum of excitement crackling in the air as the news seeped in: they had finally found not one, but two suspects, meaning they were one step closer to cracking this once unsolvable case.

"Marks, Parry; you two will chase this man down. We need to know where he has been since his was-out back in 1939." Brakes instructed before turning his attention to Ford. "Ford and Shaw, the both of you will look into this John Smith fellow—find out all that you can on him. Places of address, the aircrafts he flew... anything that might help this case. While you guys do that, I will go and find out what I can about shell shock victims."

Throwing on his coat and hat, Brakes stalked through Scotland Yard and exited the building. Once he stepped onto the streets of London, he jumped into a nearby taxi and rattled off his destination. "Guy's Hospital please, driver."

It took almost forty minutes to travel the mile or so to the hospital. The streets the driver would normally take were blocked due to bomb damaged buildings, bricks and more littering the streets. Once they arrived at their destination, Brakes exited the vehicle and promptly made his way to the reception.

"Detective Inspector Brakes," he announced, showing his identification to the receptionist. "Please can you direct me to the psychology department and tell me who heads it."

Once he had been given directions and the name of the head of the department, Brakes made his way through the hospital's labyrinth. Navigating its cluttered corridors, he saw that the hospital was spilling to breaking point with injured citizens and military personnel alike.

Eventually, Brakes arrived at the psychology department. "Excuse me," he said, stopping a matron in her tracks. "I would like to see Dr. Thomas. Could you fetch him for me or perhaps point me in the right direction to his whereabouts?”

The matron shot him a stern look, her hands pinned to her hips as she looked Brakes up and down. “You can’t just swan up here and expect to see a doctor. You must make an appointment like any other patient.” she snapped, her tone similar to that of any sergeant. “And we are on hospital grounds, sir; have some respect and remove your hat.”

Irritated, Brakes removed his hat and flashed his identity card to the woman. “Madam, I am Detective Inspector Brakes, sent by Scotland Yard.” he announced, returning the matron’s glare. “I must insist that you take me to see Dr. Thomas immediately, or I will have you arrested for obstructing a police officer in the execution of his duties.”

The matron’s face steadily grew pink, though she did not seem to lose her confidence despite her newfound embarrassment. “Follow me, sir,” she replied loudly, gesturing for Brakes to follow with her hand.

They weaved through a couple of different corridors in silence before finally arriving at Dr. Thomas’s office, where the matron finally turned back to Brakes and looked him straight in the eye. “Wait here,” she instructed him firmly before knocking on the doctor’s door.

Once she opened the door, Brakes quickly followed her into the room before she could shut him out. The matron looked alarmed but before she could utter a word, Brakes searched the room to find the man in question and raised his voice.

"Detective Inspector Brakes," he said, loud and authoritative. "Sorry to interrupt, Dr. Thomas, but I must speak with you regarding an urgent matter."

Immediately the doctor looked up, his eyes growing wide in alarm as his patient, a quiet, well-to-do young lady, flushed red at the intrusion.

"What the hell is going on here, matron?" Dr. Thomas demanded, his gaze flickering between Brakes and the undoubtedly angry matron. "This simply will not do! I have a patient. Can't this wait?" Slamming a fist down onto the desk, the doctor shot Brakes an angry glare while his patient looked between them, her face crumpling as she took in the scene before her.

Silence permeated the room until, finally, the patient mumbled something inaudible under her breath and rushed out, clearly upset as she passed Brakes by with a discerning look and a huff of annoyance, making sure to slam the door behind her.

Brakes arched a brow as he stared at the disgruntled Doctor. "Well, Doctor; it seems you have some spare time now." he said simply and took a step forward. "Let's get into why I am here, shall we?"

The doctor scowled, fixing Brakes with a cold look while he weighed his options. Then, somewhat reluctantly, the Doctor sat back down in his seat and tapped a finger against his desk.

"Very well," he said, his voice even as he kept his gaze fixed on Brakes. "Thank you, matron; that will be all." And with a dismissive wave of his other hand, the matron nodded and quickly left. Once the door was shut firmly behind her, the doctor spoke to Brakes again. "So, how may I help you, Inspector?"

Stepping further into the room, Brakes stopped just inches away from Dr. Thomas's desk. "What can you tell me about shell shock, doctor?" he asked, clasping his hands behind his back. "I am mainly interested in how it may affect someone, so there is no need for you to explain anything outside of that."

The Doctor paused for a moment, pondering Brakes' question while still tapping his finger on the desk. Sitting back in his chair, the doctor began reeling off a list of symptoms as Brakes quickly took out his notebook and pencil to write everything down.

"There are two sides to consider, Inspector," the Doctor began, his voice low. "First, there are the physical symptoms—tremors, fatigue, headaches, impaired sight and hearing, loss of balance, and difficulty with eating, drinking, and sleeping." The Doctor lifted a hand, ticking off each symptom as he said them while Brakes nodded, his pencil scratching against the notepad. The doctor paused again, waiting until Brakes had finished writing before continuing.

"Then there are the psychological symptoms. Those can include confusion, nightmares, anxiety, depression, and difficulty remembering events." Dr. Thomas explained slowly, his chair creaking slightly as he moved. "Not to mention that people suffering from shell shock can suffer from issues when reintegrating into society. Many suffer with flashbacks, which can manifest at any time."

Looking up from his notes, eyebrows pinched together, Brakes shot the doctor a curious look. "Could they be dangerous?" he asked, before clarifying: "To themselves or others, maybe?"

Dr. Thomas nodded. "Most certainly. If left untreated, the patient could become manic."

"Thank you for your time, doctor. You have been most helpful," Brakes said. Closing his notebook, he placed it back in his pocket and offered the doctor a curt not. "I will be on my way. Have a good day."

Returning his hat to his head, Brakes exited the office and made his way out of the hospital, ignoring the deliberate glare from the disgruntled matron when he passed her.

Once he was outside, Brakes decided to walk back to the station instead of flagging down a taxi. It would probably be quicker, and besides, he could use the exercise; working in his office at Scotland Yard had certainly taken priority, and Brakes hardly found time to stretch his legs or enjoy the fresh air.

As he walked, Brakes thought back to everything that he and his team had found so far.

There was now a solid connection between the two cases, as well as a probable but unconfirmed connection between Peter Hall and a new suspect, his father, Fred Hall. The man had lived in the same area of Cumbria for many years and had still been living there at the same time as when the depot break-ins had happened. The man suffered from shell shock, and his whereabouts were unknown and, though Brakes could not confirm it, it was plausible that Fred Hall could be using a pseudonym.

Of course, there was also the other suspect—the American pilot, John Smith. He had been in the vicinity of each and every murder scene during the time it happened, but little evidence had surfaced outside of that. Of course, Brakes had never really believed in coincidences, and he was certain that everything he and his team had on both Fred Hall and John Smith was enough to move forward and up his strategy in finding out who exactly was the mastermind in this grizzly series of murders.

CHAPTER SIXTEEN

As the days passed by, Brakes and his team collated all they could into one file regarding Frank Hall, John Smith and their families, as well as eliminating everyone else they could from their enquiries. By the third day, they had whittled their list down until they were left with three names, all possible suspects, but the team agreed that Fred Hall was at the top of that list.

Calling Ford to his desk, Brakes informed him that he would be returning to Cumbria, this time armed with a photo of Fred Hall.

"You will show this photo to everyone at the depot," Brakes instructed the disgruntled detective. "We need to find out if Hall worked there at any time, and if anyone recognises him. Call me immediately if you find anything."

Though Ford did not seem particularly pleased about having to return to Cumbria, especially so soon after he had returned to Scotland Yard, Brakes knew that he understood that this lead could help them conclude this case. So, without another word, Ford bade his goodbyes and left the team again to continue his investigation on Fred Hall.

There was nothing more for the team to do now but wait. He let everyone leave early but asked the remaining team members to keep a sharp ear out for their telephones, if anything were to happen.

Donning his hat and coat, Brakes left the office shortly after his team. He would take early leave, too, and perhaps give Vera a ring to see how the black-market cases were going back in Norwich.

Norwich Station

During Brakes' time in London, Vera had kept herself busy compiling a list of reported thefts, along with interviews from victims who had witnessed suspicious activity around the bombed-out buildings of Norwich.

It was on a particularly boring day when she was working on some files at her desk when the phone rang. After the second ring she picked up the receiver and pressed it to her ear.

"Constable Stanshore speaking."

A familiar voice crackled over the phone. "Vera, it's Brakes. How's things going?"

Though she was relieved to hear the detective's voice again, Vera couldn't help but frown. "It's worse than we thought, sir," she said, spreading out a series of reports in front of her. "People are taking food and supplies and, as you know, they are also targeting valuables—jewellery, heirlooms, anything that can be sold on the black market. Also, I think they're working with someone who has access to military equipment."

"What makes you say that, Vera?" Brakes asked, and she could hear the curiosity in his tone.

"Well, sir, how else would they be able to move such large amounts of stolen goods around? Civilian vehicles are subject to stop for searches, whereas military vehicles aren't." Vera explained. On the other end of the line, she heard Brakes take a sharp intake of breath as he took in her words.

"A very good point," Brakes replied, a hint of a smile in his voice. "Well spotted."

Vera felt a flutter of pride swell in her chest. "The Chief has now taken me under his wing," she informed Brakes. "He told me that he can use this opportunity as an evaluation."

"Indeed. Moreover, you will need a supervisor for certain aspects of the investigation, such as interviews and the like, Vera. There are some things you cannot do alone just yet so be sure to remember that." Brakes explained.

While she spoke with Brakes on the phone, Vera felt another presence move toward her desk. Turning, she looked up to see the Chief, his shirt sleeves rolled up, and his waistcoat unbuttoned. His eyes seemed tired but, as always, the Chief was ever-alert.

"Is that Brakes on the phone?" he asked. When Vera confirmed his question with a nod, he held out his hand and gestured for the handset before she handed it to him.

"Brakes," the Chief immediately bellowed down the phone, and Vera hoped Brakes' ears weren't ringing from the sheer force of their superior's voice.

On the other end of the line, Vera could still faintly hear Brakes' voice. "Yes, Chief?"

"I have heard good reports from the commissioner," the Chief said gruffly, his gaze turning away from Vera as she began to busy herself with some documents. "Keep it up, and please, none of your schoolboy antics whilst you're at the Yard."

They spoke for another minute while Vera looked through the black-market case files, her ears pricking up whenever her name was mentioned. There was some praise from the Chief before he was handing the phone back to her without saying goodbye to Brakes. He immediately turned to leave, his face set with determination when he turned back to Vera.

"We will be leaving in ten minutes, Stanshore. I will meet you outside with the car." he stated, walking out of the room as Vera shuffled her documents together with a nod.

"Okay, sir; I will be with you in a jiffy."

Returning the receiver to her ear, Vera heard the familiar crackle of the line as Brakes' voice filtered through it.

"You're holding your own, Vera; well done. Just keep doing what you're doing." Brakes said, and she could not help but smile at the high praise.

"Thank you, sir. I hope to see you soon, but I have to go now—don't want to keep the Chief waiting."

"I will ring again soon. Ta-ta for now." Brakes said, and the line went dead. Setting the receiver down, Vera stood and stretched before putting her files away and made her way out of the station to get the car ready for departure.

The sun was already beginning to set as Vera and the Chief made their way to a dilapidated warehouse on the outskirts of Norwich. They were hoping to find the local fence there, a man named Derek Johnson, also known as The Sea Serpent. He was known for dealing in stolen goods and had connections to various criminal elements in the area.

As they approached the entrance, a chill rippled down Vera's spine and the air surrounding her seemed to grow colder. This was not the first time she had to face a major criminal, but for some reason Vera felt uneasy. She wondered if it was due to the Chief sitting next to her, or perhaps something else was afoot.

Once she had found a parking space, Vera and the Chief jumped out of the car and started looking over the warehouse, their pistols raised in case of a surprise attack. The sky had already grown dark, the moon casting a dim glow over the building's façade. Vera shuddered.

"One would think the Sea Serpent would have his HQ closer to the docks, due to his alias." Vera thought as they cautiously approached the warehouse. The wind picked up, brushing against her skin and causing goosebumps to rise on her arms as the Chief took the lead. Vera's eyes darted this way and that, another shudder rippling through her the closer she came to the building, and she could not shake the feeling that, despite being alone with the Chief, someone was watching her.

Once they were standing in front of the building, the Chief was quick to spot a door, slightly ajar despite how late it was. With an affirming nod from her superior, Vera followed him into the quiet warehouse, the door hinges squeaking as the Chief pushed the door open a little further.

They entered a dimly lit room that smelled of damp and smoke and were immediately met with the silhouette of a figure, wiry but unmistakably masculine, sitting behind a makeshift table. He glanced up at them as they approached, caution shrouding his gaze.

"What are you doing here?" he asked, his voice gruff and low.

The Chief stepped forward while Vera stayed back, watching the exchange. "Chief Superintendent Fields. This is Constable Stanshore. We are here to see Derek Johnson." he explained curtly, cocking his pistol just so. The man simply arched a brow, his gaze falling on the barrel of the gun.

"You can holster your weapon; you're in no danger here," the man sneered. "Besides, the Serpent doesn't see anyone without an appointment, not even the police."

But the Chief didn't listen. Instead, Vera watched as he raised his sidearm and pulled back the hammer, a deafening *crack* filling the silent space. Immediately, both Vera and the Chief were surrounded without the man having to say a word, and the room was filled with the sound of at least twenty different weapons being cocked, ready to take aim and fire.

Instinctively, Vera stepped back and shrank behind the Chief, but it didn't make any difference; they were well and truly outnumbered.

"You may take us down, but I warn you; if we go, you're coming with us." the Chief snarled, his promise firm as he looked around the room, his body rigid with defiance while Vera watched quietly, her own gun raised and pointed at one of the random men in the room.

A deafening silence settled on the room, guns raised at all angles while the man behind the table simply yawned, quickly growing bored of the situation. Then, just as Vera was certain she could hear the squeeze of someone's finger against a trigger, a strong, grizzled voice rang out from above them, their presence hidden deep within shadows.

"Put your weapons down. The police mean us no harm." the voice said, rough and commanding. "You just want to talk, yes?"

Begrudgingly, the men that surrounded them began lowering their weapons, their unwavering gazes still fixed on Vera and the Chief. Slowly, the Chief began lowering his own gun and Vera quickly followed suit, her back straightening as she shot a chilling glare toward one of the men who simply grimaced back at her.

"No one wants to die today, least of all us," the Chief said, holstering his sidearm. "We just have a few simple questions, then we will be on our way."

Though neither Vera nor the Chief could see much, they could both make out that someone was making their way down the staircase. A familiar sound of hobnail boots clicked against the stairs, metal meeting metal, with the sound ringing throughout the building. Then, a *clang* and a *thump* as the heavy, metal-studded soles hit the hard surface of the concrete floor as the figure made his way toward Vera and the Chief, his soles scraping against the floor in a bid to remind them of whose domain they had entered.

When he finally stopped in front of them, his smile a twisted curve on his lips, he gestured for his men while looking between Vera and the Chief with eyes that spoke of curiosity and amusement.

"Take a seat, please," he said, and his goons quickly swarmed the room with chairs for everyone to sit on. "You will not be harmed here. You have my word."

The Chief and Vera sat cautiously around the table, watching as the man took his own seat and lit up a cigarette. Immediately, as if in tandem, the rest of the man's cronies began lighting up their own cigarettes, their faces semi-illuminated by the faint glow as the ends burned within the shadows. Taking a long drag of his cigarette, the man sat back in his chair and looked over at Vera and the Chief.

"Derek Johnson, at your service," he greeted them, his grin crooked. "Now, what can I do for you, Chief Superintendent Fields?"

The Chief did not waste any time. "We understand that you are in the import and export trade," he stated, his voice clear as Vera watched Johnson, hoping to catch any sign of a tell. "We also hear you've been moving quite a lot of... *personal* items as of late."

Johnson simply raised his eyebrows and blew out a cloud of smoke. "I don't know what you're talking about," he said with a shrug. "I'm just a humble trader trying to make a living." Taking another drag of his cigarette, Johnson shook his head. The Chief scowled, his gaze hardening at the man's calm denial.

"Don't play coy with me," the Chief said, his voice steady but firm as he leaned forward. "We also know about the stolen goods trade in the city, and that you are one of the top fences in Norwich. And if you don't want to end up in jail, I suggest you start talking."

Blowing out another cloud of smoke, Johnson sighed and sat up in his chair to meet the Chief's gaze. "Look, it's not what you think you know, it's what you can prove. I get so many people in and out of here on a daily basis, it's hard to keep up. Who is who, what is what... I don't ask questions, and I don't want to get involved in whatever you're investigating."

The Chief stiffened, and Vera knew that his patience was wearing thin. He did not like it when he had no answers and was even less tolerant of people when they avoided giving the answers he so desperately needed. A dull *thud* echoed in the room when the Chief's foot slammed against the floor, his hand curling into a fist as he let out a frustrated growl at Johnson's defiance. Leaning forward, Vera looked Johnson in the eye and tried offering her most pleasing smile in the hopes of pacifying the man enough to get a concrete answer from him.

"Listen; people are not only being bombed out of their homes, but they are also having to tolerate someone—a gang, maybe—going in and stealing all that they have left." Vera explained, her voice soft but firm as Johnson's gaze flicked over to her to show he was listening. "These poor people have been victimised enough by losing their homes, their loved ones... So, this cold, dastardly act needs to be stopped, and if you know anything about it, *anything* at all, it will help if you would let us know."

Johnson was silent as Vera said her piece and, once she had finished, he let out a grunt as he shuffled in his chair and stubbed out his dying cigarette. Lighting up a fresh one, the man took a long, slow drag from it and blew another cloud of smoke in Vera and the Chief's direction before speaking up again.

"You are welcome to come back during daylight hours. You can do all the searching you like, but I can assure you that I am not the one you are looking for." he said, a hint of annoyance lacing his voice. "You should go and speak to a man called Faulkner; he might have the answers you're looking for."

Finishing off his second cigarette, Johnson dropped it on the floor and, scraping his chair back, stood to stamp it out. When he looked back up at Vera and the Chief, his gaze had darkened considerably as his men all followed suit and dropped their own cigarettes to the floor, the ashes smouldering beneath their boots.

"Now, if you don't mind, I have things to do, so I will bid you goodnight." Turning his back on them, Johnson walked into the shadows and disappeared, the soles of his boots dragging against the concrete until neither Vera nor the Chief could hear them anymore.

As soon as Johnson had left, a single torch lit up the room, its wielder waving it to show Vera and the Chief the way out. Hesitantly, they both stood, their chairs scraping against the floor as they made their way out of the warehouse under the watchful eyes of Johnson's goons. The torch thankfully stayed lit until they had exited the building and found themselves outside again, their surroundings bathed in the weak light of the moon as they made their way back to the car.

Once they reached the vehicle, the Chief turned to Vera. "Let's call it a night, Constable Stanshore," he said tiredly, the nights events quickly weighing down on him. "We should get some sleep. We will take this up again in the morning."

Nodding, Vera opened the driver's door and slid in as the Chief took the passenger seat, shutting the door firmly behind him. Striking up the engine, she drove through the night, barely speaking a word until she finally reached the Chief's house.

"Should I pick you up in the morning or meet you at the station, sir?" she asked before he got out of the car. Opening the door, the Chief didn't turn back to look at Vera when he answered her.

"At the station, please," he replied, stepping out of the car. "09.00, sharp."

CHAPTER SEVENTEEN

Vera arrived at the station early the next morning. She needed to write up a report from the night before, as it was not only good practice to keep the files up to date, but to keep her own memory fresh on all that had happened. Besides, she needed to find something to keep her busy whilst the Chief completed his own morning duties.

By the time the Chief came to collect Vera to meet their next suspect, it was almost lunchtime, and the sky had become clouded over, a light patter of rain already beginning to fall from the heavens.

"Right, Stanshore," the Chief said, clearing his throat as Vera struck up the car. "Suspect's name is Mr. Brian Faulkner, also known as *The Grifter*. He lives at Rose Cottage, just off the main road. We're visiting him to continue our investigation into the black-market, theft of property case, yes?"

The windscreen wipers slapped a rhythmic beat against the car window, though it did little to clear the relentless drizzle that had begun to dance off the road ahead. Humming a tune that she could not quite place, Vera slid her gaze to the Chief before turning back to the road ahead.

"Sorry, sir; are you asking me or telling me?" she queried before beginning to hum again. The Chief sighed and shook his head, his frown deepening as he rubbed a hand across his forehead.

"I have so many things going around my head," he muttered tiredly. "I was just recapping, to be clear... and can you please *stop* humming?"

Vera stopped humming. "Sorry, sir. It's quite unusual, but I enjoy a good song. This one, though, I simply can't put my finger on the title, yet it has been in my head a while, now."

The Chief took a sharp intake of breath and pinched the bridge of his nose. "Look, Stanshore; just stick to the facts, alright? Keep your mind on the case and not some silly song." the Chief growled, his eyes narrowing as he turned to look at Vera. "We need to establish or see if Faulkner has any connection to this case."

"Right, sir," Vera said, her voice becoming quieter. "So, the same questions as last night, then. Hopefully this time without entering a creepy warehouse and being targeted by various goons."

"We're visiting this suspect at his home address, Stanshore, so you don't have to worry."

Vera nodded and fell quiet again, focusing on getting to their next suspect's address. Then, a thought came to her mind, and she voiced her new question to the Chief.

"So, Chief," she began, her voice bright and inquisitive, almost like a chirp that felt jarring against the grey afternoon. "About the stolen goods; do you think there's a connection to the black market?"

The Chief sighed again, this time a little heavier than before. "Stanshore," he began, warning edging his voice. "That is what we are trying to establish."

"You must try and remember, Stanshore: nothing is ever as it seems. If we are to prosecute someone, we need solid evidence." the Chief explained, quickly becoming exasperated. "Now, I know you're not new to all this police work stuff, and you have been with Brakes for over a year now. Surely, you must have picked up on the basics of police work?"

Vera hesitated, her cheer faltering at the Chief's words. "Of course, Chief. But..."

"Stanshore!" he barked, causing Vera to jump in her seat. "Enough! Just... please, for the love of all that is holy, stop bloody talking! Can we please just get to Faulkner's home without this needless chatter?"

Vera flushed, her gaze fixed squarely on the road. "Sorry, sir." she mumbled meekly. "Just thinking aloud."

Silence descended in the car for a moment, broken only by the whirr of the wipers and the patter of the rain outside. Eventually, Vera heard another haggard sigh from beside her, one that spoke of defeat.

"Stanshore, are you always like this?" the Chief asked, his voice low and soft. Vera blinked and twisted her neck to look at him and saw that his eyes were closed.

"Like what, sir?" she asked.

"This…" the Chief waved a hand in the air, as if trying to find the right words. "Relentlessly inquisitive. The incessant questioning. How exactly does DI Brakes put up with you?"

Vera blinked, taking in the questions with a furrowed brow. "DI Brakes says I have a 'thirst for knowledge' bordering on the 'utterly maddening,' sir. And sometimes 'a tendency to overthink the obvious.'" she explained.

The Chief snorted. "Brakes sounds like a bloody saint."

"He also said I'm a 'tenacious investigator' with a 'unique perspective,'" Vera added, already feeling more positive at the memory of her superior's words. The Chief grunted dismissively in response.

"Right. Well, try channelling that 'unique perspective' into silently considering your thoughts."

"Of course, sir," Vera said, snapping her mouth shut. But in less than a second, another thought crossed her mind. "Just thinking outside the box, sir. Trying to cover all the angles."

They finished the rest of the drive in silence and arrived at the Faulkner residence. Getting out of the car, the Chief knocked on the door while Vera stood behind him. They did not have to wait long when an elderly lady opened the door, her pure white hair brushed back into a tight bun and a pair of dark rimmed glasses perched at the end of her nose.

"Can I help you?" she asked cautiously, a slight whistle following her words. From her spot, Vera could see that the woman was missing several of her teeth.

"Police, madam," the Chief replied, and he and Vera showed their identification cards. "We would like to speak to Mr. Faulkner."

"He is having tea with his family in the drawing room," the woman replied, opening the door and gesturing for them to come inside. "Please, follow me."

They walked through the cottage until they came to the drawing room. Upon entering, the old woman stood by the door and announced their arrival. Stepping into the room, the Chief and Vera approached the table where Faulkner and his family were sat having afternoon tea, their eyes now fixed on the two officers that were walking towards them. Presenting their identity cards, the Chief cleared his throat.

"Just a few questions, Mr. Faulkner, and just to be clear, we can do this here, or at the station. The choice is yours." the Chief stated, leaving little room for Faulkner to reject his inevitable interrogation.

"Certainly," Faulkner replied, setting his teacup down and turning to his family. "Everyone, please be on your way; I must speak with the police." Without another word, Faulkner's family promptly left the table and exited the drawing room. The elderly woman closed the door behind her, and soon enough the room was only occupied by the Chief, Vera and Faulkner.

Even though he was seated, Vera could see that Faulkner stood at almost six-feet tall. Despite being a man in his early forties, he had jet-black hair and a build that any professional boxer would be proud of, as well as an air of nonchalance despite the position that Faulkner had presently found himself in.

"Please, sit. Would you like some tea?" Faulkner asked, waving a hand toward the now empty chairs. The Chief sat and Vera quickly followed. Opening her mouth to accept the offer of tea, Vera had barely gotten the words out when the Chief spoke up, his words rough and curt.

"We are not here to take tea." he replied, his gaze hard. Vera promptly closed her mouth, though her eyes lingered longingly on the tea pot that sat on the table.

"Then what can I do for you?" Faulkner asked, raising his brows as he looked between them both.

"Stanshore, take it from here," the Chief instructed with a wave of his hand. Nodding, Vera turned to Faulkner, whose gaze turned to her.

"Well, sir, we're looking into the theft of personal items from bombed out residences across the city. We were hoping you could shed some light on the issue?" Vera asked, pushing a plate away from her with a half-eaten scone on it.

"And why would I know anything about that?" Faulkner replied, his demeanour calm and unassuming. Vera felt the Chief stiffen beside her, his desire for answers growing and his patience rapidly dwindling.

Leaning forward, Vera narrowed her eyes in Faulkner's direction. "With all due respect, sir, everyone at this table knows who you are and what you do." Vera said, invoking an air of authority in her voice that she hoped would sway Faulkner in her favour. "So, let's stop chasing chickens and get to the crux of it all, shall we?"

At this, the Chief straightened in his chair and chimed in. "Look, Faulkner; we simply want to get to the bottom of all this. If you're not involved, then at least give us something and we can stop playing around and be on our way."

Faulkner paused, his gaze hardening as he looked between Vera and the Chief. Standing from his seat, he began pacing the room, as if deep in thought. Finally, after what seemed like a lifetime of pacing, Faulkner stopped in front of the fireplace, his back turned to Vera and the Chief. Clasping his hands behind his back, the man let out a long, thoughtful sigh before he spoke again, his voice soft but firm.

"You need to look a little closer into the ARP. That's all I will say on the matter." Faulkner murmured, his head lowering as he looked down at the burning wood in the fireplace. "Now, I will bid you a good day." Without turning back to Vera and the Chief, Faulkner gestured toward the door with his arm, a clear sign that their presence was no longer required.

Vera and the Chief took a moment to collect themselves. Standing in unison, they began making their way to leave before Vera stopped and leaned over the table. Reaching out a hand, she took hold of the largest scone topped with jam on the scone stand and brought it to her mouth before taking a large, appreciative bite. The Chief watched her as she did this, slightly bewildered before shaking his head and muttering something under his breath before heading for the door. Vera followed in hot pursuit, the scone still in her hand.

Once they were outside, Vera pushed the rest of the scone into her mouth before getting into the car. Wiping her hands quickly, she put on her gloves and jumped into the driver's seat.

"Looks like you enjoyed that scone, Constable." the Chief sneered, sliding into the passenger seat as he focused on her face. Vera had the decency to blush and offered the Chief a small shrug.

"Sorry, Chief; I was starving." she replied. The Chief simply tutted and shook his head again.

"Well, you have jam all over your face. Clean yourself up." the Chief grumbled, turning his gaze to the window as Vera quickly pulled off her gloves and started checking herself in the rear-view mirror. Seeing the sticky jam smeared across her lips and cheeks, Vera grabbed a handkerchief and quickly cleaned herself up. Once she was done, she replaced her gloves and put her hands on the wheel.

"To one of the ARP stations then, sir?" she asked, starting up the car and awaiting the Chief's instruction. He was quiet for a moment, sitting with his thoughts before he spoke again.

"Turn off the engine a moment, Constable." the Chief instructed, and Vera did as she was told. "Now, if my memory is correct, you and Brakes interviewed several ARP stations, yes?"

"Yes, sir." Vera confirmed.

"Did any of them stand out? Did any one of them look the slightest bit shifty?" he queried, his eyes hard. "Was there anyone that Brakes thought deserved further investigation?"

Vera nodded. "Oh, yes, there were a few that stood out," she replied confidently, remembering the men that she and Brakes had first encountered. "One of the stations had some very shifty characters working there."

"Then that will be our first stop."

Vera started the car again and headed off to the quarry where the ARP station that she and Brakes had first visited was situated. It was getting late in the day, which meant that the shift change was imminent, and if Vera's memory was correct, that meant the fella's she and Brakes had initially talked to would just be coming on shift.

"Park up somewhere where we can observe the quarry without detection." the Chief instructed once they had arrived, his gaze sweeping over the scene before him. Vera nodded, turning off the engine and taking off her driving gloves.

"What are we doing, sir?" she asked, placing her gloves on the dashboard. Out of the corner of her eye, she caught sight of three familiar figures in the distance—Frankie, Tony and Mikey, the men that she and Brakes had talked to—and a fourth person, someone she did not recognise. Pointing out the window, she said, "The men are right there, in the street. Let's go get them."

Vera reached for the door handle, but a quick shake of the Chief's head stopped her. "Hold your horses, Stanshore," he commanded, his own gaze turning to the men on the street. "Look at them—it seems that they are arguing about something. Let's just wait and see how this plays out."

Turning back to the window, Vera could see that the men were all pushing and shoving each other, their voices increasingly rising in a bid to be heard over the others. After a few short moments, a light scuffle broke out between them, with each of the men jockeying for position in a bid to gain the upper hand.

"Something is certainly wrong here, Stanshore." the Chief murmured, his eyes fixed on the scene before him. "They have started to fight each other, can you see?"

Squinting her eyes, Vera watched the scuffle and found that she did not agree with the Chief. "Sorry, sir, but that's not really a fight," she said, leaning forward as the men tugged and pushed each other. A smile formed on her lips. "This looks more like a bunch of women trying to catch a wedding bouquet."

The Chief frowned in response. "Well, I can agree to that; they are certainly not professionally trained fighters."

Vera and the Chief continued to watch the men in silence. After a few minutes the men finally broke it up, mostly because they had come to realise that they were attracting unwanted attention from the local residents. Once they had dusted themselves off, Vera and the Chief watched as the four men walked inside the station.

"Shall we go in now, sir?" Vera asked, turning to the Chief who simply shook his head.

"Not yet. Let's give them a moment or two to calm down and settle in for the night." he said, watching the now empty space before them, in case the men might reappear. After a moment of silence, he finally added, "You must develop a sense of patience in this job, Constable."

Just as the Chief finished speaking, two beat bobbies appeared from around the corner. Every few moments they stopped to talk to the residents standing around the street, their faces hardened and serious.

"It looks like someone phoned the police, sir. Due to the ruckus, I expect." Vera said. From her periphery, she saw the Chief nod.

"It would seem so," the Chief agreed, his frown deepening. "Stanshore, flash your headlights at them until you get their attention; we don't want them going into the ARP station just yet."

As instructed, Vera began flashing the car headlights on and off. After a moment or two, the police officers caught sight of the action and began making their way over to the car, which Vera knew they would immediately recognise as a local police vehicle.

Once they had stopped in front the car, the Chief stepped out and greeted the two men. "Officers," he said, offering them both a nod. "Constable Stanshore and I are currently looking into the black-market case, though we believe something more sinister is afoot. We need to arrest these men for questioning regarding some recent thefts. I also need you to take up position down the road and potentially cut off anyone who might make a run for it."

As Vera stepped out of the car from the driver's side, the two officers were already agreeing to the Chief's orders with stiff, resolute nods.

"We will stand watch from the car. I advise that neither of you move until you see me or Constable Stanshore move into the station." the Chief instructed the officers, his eyes dark and posture rigid as the men nodded again. "Once we are inside, follow us in. I am certain we will need backup."

With the officers keeping watch for any runners, Vera and the Chief returned to the car and continued to observe the station. Few words passed between them as the hours ticked by until finally, when the day had faded into the night, they caught sight of two shadowy figures coming out of the ARP station, both carrying what Vera could only describe as thin pieces of iron bar.

"What do you think they are up to, Chief?" Vera asked, watching as the men began walking down the street.

"Who knows. Something is certainly going on here, though." the Chief replied, his brow wrinkling as he squinted at the figures, barely visible under the cover of the night. "Sit tight, Stanshore; let's see what they're up to."

It didn't take too long for the men to stop in the middle of the road. One of them bent down, though neither Vera nor the Chief could make out he was doing. A moment later however, the man stood up and both men took hold of their iron bars and proceeded to lift a manhole cover that led to the sewers.

Vera held her breath. One of the two figures knelt down and, from where she sat, she could make out the shadow of what looked like a large sack being pulled from the manhole before quickly replacing the cover, and the two men quickly made their way back into the station with the newly acquired sack.

Once they were certain the men were no longer on the street, the Chief turned to Vera, his face set with determination. "Right, Stanshore; we will now be heading inside. Once we get close to the station, I want you to blow your whistle as loud as you can. It will alert the other officers."

"Understood, sir." Vera replied and without hesitation, she exited the car and followed the Chief toward the ARP station. They crept through the cover of darkness, their sidearms raised and making sure to keep quiet so as not to alert their suspects. However, as they came to the door of the station they were met with one of the men.

A larger set fellow, Vera did not immediately recognise him, but it was clear he knew that they were with the police. His beady, black eyes bore into them as he stood tall, the sack in his hand now swinging wildly around his head as his lips curled into a ferocious snarl.

"You'll never take me alive, copper!" he bellowed, bringing the sack down in the Chief's direction. Vera gasped, but her superior was far quicker than their assailant; dodging the heavy sack, the Chief hurtled forward, his arms wrapping around the man's large waist. With a hefty *"Oof,"* and a deafening *thud*, the man was quickly wrestled to the ground.

"Stop! Police!" Vera roared and brought the whistle to her lips. A deafening shriek filled the quiet of the night and the other three men—Frankie, Tony and Mikey, she realised—started scrambling around the yard looking panicked as they searched for an exit.

Soon enough, the other two officers had arrived on the scene and along with Vera, they ran after the men, wrestling two to the ground while the last one— Mikey, the youngest of the four—weaved past them, far too quick and nimble to be caught. Gritting her teeth, Vera gave chase, her feet pounding against the ground while her heartbeat thrummed in her ears. She would *not* let this man go, not when Brakes relied so heavily on her to continue this case.

Vera bolted towards the young man, turning corners and skidding across the floor, but he proved to be too fast. Sweat beaded at her brow, her breath becoming laboured as the lad kept looking over his shoulder, his face red and eyes wide with fear. Then, Vera saw it: an exit ahead of them, a means for the young man to escape. "*Bloody Hell*," she cursed under her breath, knowing full well that if she did not catch him, the lad would most certainly escape her clutches.

Except as they got closer, Vera realised that the exit was, in fact, blocked. There, forming an impenetrable wall stood a crowd of residents, their faces hardened as the young man, realising his own fate far too late, ricocheted into them, his shout of protest swallowed by the roar of the men that begun grabbing and shoving him to the ground.

Slowing to a jog, Vera took a gulp of air as she made her way toward the crowd. It seemed her whistleblowing had helped, alerting the residents to the police's plight, and now they had managed to capture one of the thugs for her. Pushing her way through the huddle of bodies, Vera reached for the lad and cuffed him. With the help of the men in the crowd, they brought the young man to his feet.

"Thank you for your help," she said to the crowd, and began frog-marching the lad back to the others, who had all been cuffed and were now being held back by the Chief and the other two officers.

Soon enough, the night air was alive with the piercing sounds of police sirens and in no time at all, all four of the men they had captured were placed in separate police cars.

As the police kept watch on the men in the cars, Vera and the Chief stayed back in the ARP station to look through the sack. Bending down, the Chief opened it up and emptied the contents onto the floor. There, glinting beneath the light were the personal items that had been stolen from the bombed-out houses.

"Oh, my," Vera gasped, clamping a hand to her mouth as an unpleasant, pungent smell invaded the air. "That smells like sh-"

"That, Constable, is your evidence." the Chief said, cutting Vera off before she could finish her sentence. "Now, pack it up and get those men back to the station and book them. Congratulations on completing your first case."

Standing straight, the Chief started making his way out the door. Turning sharply on the spot, Vera stared back at him, wide-eyed and pale, her hand still covering her mouth.

"But, sir," she protested, her voice growing shrill. "Do you have gloves? It smells!"

The Chief simply laughed. "Well, you know what they say: where there's muck, there's brass, lass." And with a final bark of laughter, the Chief exited the station and loudly instructed everyone to return the station as Vera turned back to the evidence, her stomach beginning to churn uncomfortably.

CHAPTER EIGHTEEN

Back in London.

A couple of days had passed. Ford had returned once more from Cumbria, but this time with actual evidence.

"Statements from the military depot." he announced, throwing the papers onto Brakes' desk. "Six or so of them, though it might surprise you what they all said."

Grabbing the papers, Brakes quickly scanned through the contents, his eyes narrowed, and brows pinched together. Immediately, he saw what Ford was talking about: in each and every statement, the same thing came up again and again.

Fred Hall was, in fact, John Smith.

"I did not need to ask them any questions," Ford explained, his hands clasped behind his back as he watched Brakes read through the files. "Once they saw the photo, they said, 'That's John Smith' and refused to believe that his real name was Fred Hall."

"So, we are searching for one man." Brakes murmured, his heart hammering against his chest. They were now one step closer to finding their man, and even closer to completing this case. Throwing down the statements, Brakes leaned over the desk to grab the phone.

"Gather everyone together; I need the teams full attention. But first, I have to make a call." he said, his voice low as he dialled the number he needed. Pressing the receiver to his ear, the phone rang twice before someone picked up.

Briefly and urgently, Brakes explained the situation and that he would need to make use of an RAF outpost. "We need to search for a rogue Spitfire," he explained. "It is imperative that we make use of the radar system to track this man down, and urgently... Yes. Yes, thank you for time." Slamming the phone down, Brakes dialled another number and requested two cars and some backup to meet them outside before finally turning to his team. Standing from his chair, each one of them looked back at him expectantly.

"Everyone, listen up! We need to stop this man before he hurts anyone else. Follow me!" he barked and without another word, everyone filed out of the room, their work abandoned as they followed Brakes through Scotland Yard. Once they were outside in the brisk London air, Brakes led them to the cars that were waiting for them and told the drivers the address they would be heading to, followed by a few extra police cars in case anything happened.

Soon enough, Brakes and his team had commandeered a nearby ramshackle RAF radio outpost. Its lone operator hunched over the dials under Brakes' scrutiny, scouring frequencies for whispers of a rogue Spitfire slicing through the skies without a flight plan.

Day bled into night, the tension gnawing at their nerves. The team took turns lingering in the suffocating room, but after twenty minutes at a time spent in the room, the stale air and relentless static drove even the hardiest souls back outside to the crisp Suffolk night air.

Then, a crackle shattered the monotony.

"Brakes!" the operator's snapped, his voice taut with urgency. "Unidentified aircraft, no IFF signal. Took off from an Oxford airstrip an hour ago, vectoring east—straight for Suffolk."

Suffolk. The epicentre of the latest parachute murder. Brakes' pulse hammered, icy dread coiling in his gut. Grabbing a nearby phone and frantically dialling, the person on the other end had barely picked up when he roared, "Operation Nightingale, now! All radar stations, lock on that Spitfire. Patch me through to the nearest anti-aircraft battery!"

He spun to his team, eyes blazing. "Hall is in the air. We move—now!"

Engines roared as their convoy tore across the darkened countryside, headlights carving through mist-shrouded lanes. Above, the unseen Spitfire prowled, piloted by the elusive Fred Hall, the phantom behind the Parachute Murders and the chilling 'Sock Murders'. Brakes' jaw clenched; this was their shot to end his reign of terror.

Brakes and the team arrived at London airfield where the Chief Superintendent had a plane standing by for them, a respectable Lysander that would aid them in their chase. The pilot, an RAF veteran named Hawkins, had already been briefed and was in constant contact with the ground crew who were tracking Hall.

"Ford, Marks, you will be coming with me," Brakes instructed his team, his face set with determination. "Parry and Shaw, you will both stay on ground with the operators. Be ready for when we catch Hall."

One by one, Brakes, Ford, Marks and their pilot entered the aircraft and strapped in, adjusting their headsets and within minutes, they were already in the air and in hot pursuit of the rogue Spitfire.

A second call crackled through the headset. "Sir!" the operator's voice trembled. "Reports of ground fire targeting the aircraft—.50-calibre Vickers bursts. They're not aiming to kill, just... goading it."

Brakes' eyes narrowed. ".50-calibre isn't a bloody prank—it's a death sentence with bad aim." Who was firing? A rival hunter? A taunt from Hall's warped playbook? The questions burned, but there was no time to unravel them.

The unarmed Lysander's engine hummed beneath Brakes as it clawed through the Suffolk night. Strapped into the cramped cockpit, his team huddled in tense silence, headsets crackling with updates from the ground crew tracking Hall's rogue Spitfire. The plane shuddered, climbing into the inky sky, every vibration amplifying the stakes. Somewhere ahead, Fred Hall wove through the clouds, his Spitfire a lethal shadow.

"Ground control, any fix on him?" Brakes' voice cut through the static, sharp and urgent.

"Target's five miles east, altitude 3,000 feet, erratic course," the operator replied, voice taut. "He's dodging the radar like he knows we're coming."

Brakes' jaw tightened. Hall was no amateur. The Lysander's pilot nudged the throttle, coaxing every ounce of speed from the sluggish aircraft. "He's got us outgunned and outmanoeuvred." Hawkins muttered. "This crate's no match for a Spitfire."

"Then we outsmart him," Brakes shot back, eyes scanning the void beyond the cockpit glass. The moon broke through scattered clouds, casting a ghostly glow over patchwork fields below. Somewhere in that darkness, Hall was waiting.

A sudden burst of static erupted in their headsets. "Ground fire reported again!" the operator barked. ".50-calibre Vickers, sporadic bursts. Still not aiming to kill—just harassing him."

Ford leaned forward, his face pale. "Who the hell's shooting? And why aren't they finishing the job?"

"No time for theories," Brakes snapped. "Hawkins, get us closer. We need eyes on him."

The Lysander banked sharply, its engines straining as it chased the ghost of Hall's Spitfire. Then, a glint of metal flashed in the moonlight—a sleek, predatory shape slicing through the sky.

"There!" Marks shouted, pointing. The Spitfire's silhouette was unmistakable, its Merlin engine snarling in defiance.

"He's seen us," Hawkins growled, his knuckles white on the controls. Before anyone could react, the Spitfire rolled into a vicious dive, its nose aimed straight at them. Twin streams of tracer fire erupted from its wings, carving molten arcs through the night. The Lysander lurched as Hawkins yanked the stick, dodging an onslaught of bullets by inches.

"Hold on!" Brakes roared, gripping the seat as the plane twisted violently. Hall was relentless, pulling up only to loop back, his Spitfire dancing with lethal precision. The cat-and-mouse chase ignited a heart-pounding duel in the sky. The Lysander, painfully slow and defenceless, weaved desperately as Hall's guns blazed again, stitching the darkness with fire. A glancing hit sparked off the wing, the impact jarring the cabin.

"He's toying with us!" the pilot yelled, his voice cracking as another burst of bullets narrowly missed them, the shockwave rattling their bones.

"Keep him in sight!" Brakes ordered, sweat now beading on his brow. Hawkins pushed the Lysander into a shallow dive, skimming treetops to shake Hall's aim. The Spitfire followed, relentless. Every manoeuvre was a gamble, every second a brush with death. Hall's gunfire roared again, tearing through the Lysander's tail and sending shrapnel pinging through the fuselage. Warning lights flared on the dashboard.

"She's hit bad!" Hawkins shouted, wrestling the controls as the plane shuddered violently. "Losing hydraulics—we can't keep this up!"

Brakes' mind raced. They were unarmed and outclassed, but he wouldn't let Hall slip away. "Stay on him!" he barked, even as the Spitfire swung wide, preparing for another deadly pass. The Lysander groaned, smoke trailing from its wounded tail, but Hawkins coaxed it into a desperate climb, buying them precious seconds.

Then, disaster. Hall's next volley struck true, shredding the Lysander's left engine. The plane bucked, spiralling downward as flames licked the wing. "Brace!" Hawkins bellowed, fighting to level the descent. Brakes, Ford and Marks clung to anything solid, the world a blur of screaming wind and roaring fire. Below, a patchwork field rushed up to meet them and for a moment, all Brakes could hear were his teams terrified screams.

The impact was chaos—metal crumpled, earth tore, and the Lysander skidded across the muddy field. Pain soared through Brakes' bones, his ears ringing in the aftermath, his throat sore. Silence followed, broken only by the hiss of steam and the distant drone of Hall's Spitfire vanishing into the night. Brakes coughed, blood trickling from a gash on his forehead. A searing pain shot through the arm he had landed on, blood already beginning to run down his hand as his shirt stuck to the newly opened wound. Gritting his teeth, Brakes sat up and gripped hold of his wounded arm as his team groaned all around him, taking in the wreckage that now

surrounded them. Yet as he looked around, Brakes'
eyes burned with resolve.

They were down, battered but alive. Hall had
won this round, but the hunt was far from over.

Several sets of headlights headed for the crash
site. Keeping their distance in case of an explosion,
they came to a holt. Brakes quickly checked on the
team, all of them a little bloodied and bruised, but
undoubtedly alive.

"Everyone, out!" the pilot screamed,
scrambling out of his seat.

Coughing and wiping blood from their faces,
Brakes, Ford, Marks and Hawkings stumbled out of
the burning aircraft, their eyes searing from smoke.
Those on the ground quickly offered them water and
did their best to administer first aid with what they
had, and everyone was soon patched up. It wasn't long
after that that a couple of RAF jeeps arrived on the
scene.

"Which one of you is Inspector Brakes?" one of
the drivers yelled. Slowly, Brakes made his way
towards the jeep.

"I'm Brakes." he stated. The driver nodded.

"You're needed on the radio, sir. Here you go."
he said, passing Brakes a handset. Immediately, a
voice crackled to life, the words urgent.

"Ground radar control here, sir." the voice stated over the radio. "We have our sights on Hall. He is about eight miles due south of your position."

"Keep tracking him," Brakes ordered, his mind a storm of calculations. Passing the handset back to the driver, Brakes turned to team of people behind him, their faces a mixture of curiosity and trepidation. "Right, team; we still have him. Anyone wish to join me in catching this bastard?"

He didn't have to ask twice. A chorus of agreement echoed around the illuminated field, and the team began piling into the jeeps before speeding off again in pursuit of their prey.

The convoy screamed toward Suffolk's open fields, the tires chewing gravel. It wasn't long before Brakes saw a shadow slice across the moonlit sky. The Spitfire's silhouette was unmistakable, its Merlin engine snarling against the quiet night. Hall had got them in his sights once again; he must have been watching them from a safe distance.

"Get down!" Brakes bellowed as the plane banked hard, diving toward the convoy with lethal intent. The night erupted in chaos once again—twin streams of tracer fire tore from the Spitfire's wings, stitching the ground with deafening roars. Dirt exploded around the lead car, shrapnel pinging off the metal as Brakes' jeep swerved, his heart pounding. The team scattered, jeep tires screeching as Hall pulled up, the Spitfire's scream fading only to loop back for another pass.

"He's toying with us!" Ford shouted, gripping the seat in front of him. The driver floored the accelerator, weaving through a hail of bullets. The ground shuddered under the onslaught, each burst closer, more precise. Hall wasn't just harassing them—he was hunting.

Then, they saw it: a tunnel emerging out of the darkness, illuminated by the jeep's lights. A sanctuary that would offer them coverage and hide them out of sight and, more importantly, out of the range of the Spitfire's guns.

The driver took them into the tunnel just far enough, hidden from view but still in the vicinity of the entrance so that Brakes and his team could see outside. One by one the other jeeps crawled into the space, their engines falling quiet and the headlights dying out. Above, they could still hear the Spitfire overhead, circling the skies.

"He can't get to us in here, sir." the driver panted, killing the engine.

"Thank bloody God," Marks muttered, shaking her head wearily. "I have just about had enough of this. In fact, I could use a stiff drink right about now."

"Well, it just so happens I have exactly what you need," laughed the driver, and he promptly pulled out of a bottle of scotch he had stashed away. "I was saving this for the weekend with my special girl, but I believe the current situation calls for a spot of scotch, don't you?"

With a low whistle, the driver signalled for everyone else to come join them. A chorus of slamming doors echoed throughout the tunnel and soon enough, all of the other drivers and passengers joined Brakes' teams' jeep. Stepping out of the vehicle, Brakes' team and everyone else huddled around the jeep in complete darkness. Passing the scotch around their makeshift circle, everyone took turns swigging from the bottle while the Spitfire sputtered outside.

"The Spitfire carries around two thousand rounds. Eight guns with three hundred and fifty rounds each." One of the RAF men piped before taking another drink of the burning scotch. "They fire their .303 rounds at a rate of over one thousand rounds per minute. At the rate he has been firing, he must be almost out of rounds. He will certainly not be able to circle about out there for too much longer; he will be getting low on fuel with all the antics he has been pulling."

The bottle began making its way around the group again as everyone murmured in agreement, still listening out for the Spitfire. It took another twenty minutes or so before they finally heard the Merlin engine melting into the distance. Taking one last mouthful of scotch, Brakes handed the bottle to someone on his left and wiped his mouth with the back of his hand.

"He must be going to land somewhere, sir," Brakes' driver said, his voice a hushed whisper as he turned back to the jeep. "I will radio control and ask them to get a fix on him for you. For now, though, it might be best to follow our target; he can't stay up in the sky forever."

Turning back to the jeep, the driver made the call to radio control, his instructions brief and curt. Then he was turning back to everyone and barking orders for them to get back in their vehicles. Like ants, everyone quickly filed into their respective jeeps, the doors slamming almost simultaneously. With a curt nod, the driver struck up his engine and, one by one, the vehicles trickled out of the tunnel into the dark of the night, following the path of the Spitfire.

As the quiet hum of jeep engines echoed through the night, Brakes and his team found themselves in total silence while they impatiently awaited the answer to the radio call.

CHAPTER NINETEEN

It took far longer than Brakes had thought, but eventually the radio crackled into life once more.

"He has gone down north of Chelmsford, sir. You will need to search a five-mile radius though, because that's as close as we can get you." the voice stated, causing Brakes to frown.

"Understood. Now, I need you contact Scotland Yard. Ask to speak to the Chief Superintendent and give him this message, please: 'Contact Chelmsford station; ask them to rally every man they have and search the area given to you by the RAF control. They are looking for a private airstrip. Ask them not to move in if they find anything, but to contact Detective Inspector Brakes on this frequency immediately.'" Brakes said, his voice low and filled with urgency as he spoke into the radio. A beat of silent filled the air, stifling as he waited for the operator to answer.

"Yes, sir, right away," the voice finally confirmed, and the radio line quickly went dead.

"It will take us about two hours to get there, Inspector," the driver informed him, his brows furrowed as Brakes turned to him with a scowl.

"Then get your bloody foot down, man! We have a madman to stop!" Brakes snapped, his pulse racing at the thought of potentially losing Hall, who seemed so close yet so far from their grasp.

The RAF jeeps were much slower than a police car, and a lot more uncomfortable to sit in. The noise from the knobbly tires was incredibly loud, and it was clear that the vehicles had been made for off-road use, but it was all Brakes had right now, and despite the discomfort, he was thankful for having the jeeps at his disposal.

The miles and time passed by at a solid rate, and the vehicle was filled with silence and determination to get to their destination. Soon enough, there was only forty minutes left before they reached Chelmsford and the area that they needed to be in to finally catch Hall.

The night pulsed as the stars in the sky faded out and the sun began its rise. Urgency surged through Brakes and his team while they drove when, in the distance, they saw over thirty police officers already waiting for them—local constables, RAF auxiliaries and more. From the moment he saw them, Brakes could not help but grin.

The jeep rushed toward the crowd that had gathered around the remote Suffolk airstrip. Tires screeched over rutted lanes, kicking up clouds of dust that swirled in the glow of headlight from the following vehicle. They were close, Brakes thought; Hall was about to be cornered, but that made him no less dangerous. Heart hammering in his chest, Brakes clutched at his throbbing, bloodied arm and swallowed thickly. Hall was now within reach, and he knew deep down that this could finally be the end of the Parachute Murderer and the phantom behind the 'Sock Murders' that had haunted the police for years.

They pulled up in a cloud of dust and Brakes immediately jumped out. "Right lads, gather round," he barked, waving over the officers that were milling about. Once they approached, Brakes asked, "What have you got?"

The local inspector walked forward and immediately pulled a map out of his coat. Placing it on the jeeps bonnet, the inspector leaned in, his voice low as he pointed to the map. "Okay, listen up: this is the only farm with a grass airstrip. It is approximately two miles down this road."

With the tip of his finger, the inspector circled the position on the map. Nodding, Brakes turned back to the police that had congregated around him and raised his voice authoritatively.

"Right, everyone, listen up! The man we are after is one Fred Hall. Alias: John Smith. He is an accomplished ex-soldier from World War One, so you should under no circumstances underestimate this man. He is dangerous, and I would like to take him alive if possible. If you have to defend yourselves, however, then do so." Brakes began pacing the area, his hands clasped tightly behind his back as he looked each officer in the face before continuing. "Understood? Okay. Let's go, and quietly, please."

Everybody moved in tandem, some towards their vehicles, others following Brakes as he led the way, uniform and silent as the sun rose higher on the horizon. The farmhouse loomed ahead, a squat structure with a weathered silhouette that sat against the morning sky. Its windows flickered with the unsteady glow of lamplight while a dirt track snaked from the house to the airstrip. There the Spitfire sat, slightly hidden by the barn that it had been backed into, its sleek form a predator at rest while the wings glinted faintly beneath the pale light of the morning sun.

Once they were close enough, Brakes raised a clenched fist, signalling the convoy to halt. Engines idled, their low rumble blending with the chirp of morning chorus and the distant hoot of an owl.

Scanning the terrain, Brakes' eyes narrowed at the hedgerows and dry-stone walls that flanked the approach. "He's in there," Brakes whispered to those that had followed him on foot. Reaching a hand into his coat, his grip tightened around his Webley revolver, the cold metal grounding his resolve. "Fan out, silent approach. No mistakes. And someone go and disable that Spitfire; if Hall gets off the ground, he will cause some serious damage."

The officers dispersed like spectres, their dark uniforms melding with the shadows cast by the rising sun as they wove through gnarled bushes and low walls. The air was thick with the promise of violence, each step tightening the coil of tension in Brakes' chest. Leading Marks and Ford toward the farmhouse's rear, their breaths shallow, the three of them spear-headed the hunt for Hall.

Marks, wiry and quick, clutched her service pistol, her eyes darting to every shadow with each step. Ford carried an Enfield rifle, his jaw set against the weight of their near-miss with death. They crept closer to the farmhouse when a twig snapped under Brakes' boot and he froze, heart slamming against his ribs, but the farmhouse remained silent, the sun's rays illuminating the two rooms at the back of the house, steady, but betraying nothing.

The house's weathered timbers loomed above them like a fortress. Brakes' pulse roared in his ears, the memory of Hall's Spitfire strafing their Lysander still vivid. Hall was no ordinary killer; he was a master of chaos, a man who'd turned parachutes into murder weapons and left socks as macabre calling cards. This was their chance to end him, but Brakes knew one misstep could turn the hunter into the hunted.

Then, chaos erupted. A second-floor window shattered, the glass exploding outward, followed by the sharp crack of a Lee-Enfield rifle tearing through the night. Hall had spotted them.

"Down!" Brakes roared, diving behind a low stone wall as bullets ripped through the air, splintering a nearby fence and kicking up clouds of dirt. Officers scattered, their disciplined formation fracturing under the onslaught. Muzzle flashes lit the darkness in the room, and the answering bark of police pistols and Enfield's filled the air with a cacophony of war. Hall, silhouetted in the upstairs window, wielded his rifle with lethal precision, each shot a calculated strike that pinned the advancing force.

"He's got us in a kill zone!" Ford shouted, ducking as a round grazed the wall, showering him with jagged stone chips. Brakes pressed himself into the mud as his mind began to race. Hall's gunfire was unrelenting, a relentless barrage that forced the officers to crawl or hunker behind meagre cover. Constables fired back, their bullets chipping at the farmhouse's facade, but Hall's elevated position gave him the advantage, his shots cutting down anyone who dared advance too far.

In the distance, a constable screamed. Brakes turned to the chilling sound and saw the young man clutching his shoulder, blood blooming through his uniform. Brakes' stomach twisted; they were losing ground.

"We can't stay pinned!" Brakes hissed, his voice barely audible over the gunfire. He locked eyes with Ford, his face a mask of determination as he nodded. "Flank him," Brakes ordered, gesturing toward the rear of the house. "Marks, you're with me. Front squad, draw his fire!"

A group of officers surged toward the front door, their pistols blazing to keep Hall's attention. And the distraction worked—Hall's rifle swung toward the assault, giving Brakes and his team a fleeting window. They sprinted through the shadows, skirting the farmhouse's side where ivy clung to the crumbling bricks. The rear door, weathered and half-rotted, stood unguarded. Brakes didn't hesitate. He drove his boot into the wood, splintering it with a single, thunderous kick. The door gave way, revealing a dim interior that reeked of oil, cordite and stale tobacco.

The corridors were a maze of shadows, lit only by the faint glow of a single oil lamp. Footsteps thundered above—Hall was on the move.

Brakes led the charge, his revolver raised with Marks following close behind. The creaking stairs groaned under their weight, each step a heartbeat in the suffocating silence between gunshots.

The air grew heavier, thick with the tang of gunpowder and the weight of impending violence. They reached the landing where a narrow hallway led to a closed door, light seeping from beneath it. Looking around, Brakes saw that Ford and his team were close behind them and signalled for silence. He nodded first to Marks and then to Ford, who shouldered his Enfield, ready to breach.

They burst into the room just as Hall spun around, his Lee-Enfield blazing. A bullet grazed Brakes' injured arm, the pain like a white-hot blade, but he lunged forward, driven by fury and instinct. He tackled Hall to the floor, the rifle skidding across the warped boards with a clatter. The two grappled in a frenzy, Hall's wiry strength surprising for a man who'd not only spent hours in the air but was also of a certain age where his strength should have been in decline.

Hall's eyes burned with wild desperation, teeth bared as he clawed for leverage. Brakes slammed a fist into his targets jaw, but the killer twisted free, rolling to his knees and drawing a concealed Luger from his belt just moments before a cacophony of shouts echoed throughout the house, quickly followed by a thunder of footsteps on the floorboards.

Officers flooded in one by one, their shouts mingling with the deafening crack of gunfire. Hall began firing wildly, the Luger's muzzle flashing, but a constable's revolver found him first. A bullet punched through Hall's shoulder, blood spraying across the wall as he staggered. Before he could recover, a second shot tore through his leg, dropping him to the floor with a guttural scream that echoed in the cramped space. The Luger fell from his grasp, spinning uselessly across the floor.

"Hold fire!" Brakes bellowed, clutching his wounded arm as a fresh wave of blood soaked through his sleeve. The officers surged forward, pinning Hall to the ground. He thrashed around like a cornered beast, spitting curses, his face contorted with a mixture of pain and defiance.

"Cuff him!" Brakes ordered, his voice raw. A constable snapped heavy irons on Hall's wrists, the metal clicking shut with finality. Blood pooled beneath him, staining the floorboards, but his chest still rose and fell, his breathing ragged. Brakes towered over him, his own pain forgotten in the heat of victory.

"Fred Hall, alias John Smith," he panted, "you're under arrest for murder."

Hall's lips curled into a weak, venomous sneer. "You think this ends it?" he rasped, his voice thick with pain. "You've no idea what's coming." The words hung in the air, but Brakes dismissed them as the ravings of a broken man. The officers hauled Hall to his feet, his wounded leg dragging and his shoulder leaking crimson. A field medic, part of the RAF contingent, rushed forward, staunching the wounds just enough to keep Hall alive for the journey to custody.

Brakes stepped back, his chest heaving as the room buzzed with activity. Constables secured the scene, their lanterns casting stark shadows across the walls that revealed maps, parachutes, and a grisly collection of socks pinned to a board—Hall's twisted trophies. Walking up behind Brakes, Ford wiped the sweat from his brow with the back of his hand.

"Bloody hell, sir," he muttered, his eyes scanning the walls. "We got him." Still clutching his Enfield, Ford finally turned to Brakes and gave a curt nod before quickly scanning the room for any lingering threat.

"Sir, you're hurt!" Marks cried out, coming up beside Brakes as she looked over his arm with wide eyes. Brakes simply waved her off with his good hand.

"It's nothing, just a graze." he replied, exhausted and in pain. Slowly, Brakes allowed himself to slump against the wall until he fell crumpled to the ground, a tight smile on his lips. "We got him, Marks. We finally got him."

Outside, the Suffolk morning had fallen quiet, the firefighter's echoes fading into the wind that rustled through the fields. Brakes stepped onto the porch, the cool air a balm against his burning arm.

The Spitfire sat silent in the barn while officers milled about, their voices low as they processed the toll of the night's events. Two constables had been wounded, one seriously, but none were lost—a small miracle in the face of Hall's ferocity.

Brakes lit a cigarette, the flare faint against the morning light. The weight of the 'Parachute' and 'Sock Murders' had finally lifted, if only slightly, and was quickly replaced by a grim satisfaction. Hall was theirs, his reign of terror having ended in a haze of gunpowder and sweat, but his final words gnawed at Brakes—what did he mean, *"What's coming"*? Was it a bluff, or did Hall have accomplices still lurking in the shadows of wartime Britain? The thought sent a shiver down Brakes' spine, but he pushed it aside. For now, justice had its grip on Fred Hall.

Brakes watched as the convoy reformed, and Hall was loaded into an armoured van under heavy guard. The vehicle rumbled down the dirt track as Ford and Marks joined him on the porch, their faces etched with exhaustion but glowing with the quiet pride of victory.

As silence fell upon them, Ford cleared his throat and turned to Brakes. "Back to London, then?" he asked, his voice hoarse.

Brakes nodded, exhaling a plume of smoke. "Back to London. But this isn't over; not yet." He glanced back at the farmhouse, its lamplight now extinguished. The Parachute Murders were solved, but the war and its secrets stretched on.

CHAPTER TWENTY

The journey back to London was a blur of exhaustion and muted triumph. The convoy rolled through the sun-drenched countryside, the Suffolk fields giving way to the sprawling outskirts of the capital where the scars of the Blitz still lingered in shattered brick and twisted iron. Brakes sat in the lead car, his arm throbbing beneath a hastily applied bandage, the pain a dull counterpoint to the adrenaline still coursing through his veins. Ford and Marks were slumped beside him, their faces drawn and eyes heavy with tiredness while the armoured van carrying Fred Hall rumbled ahead.

Brakes stared out the window, the cigarette he'd lit at the farmhouse long since burned to ash. Scotland Yard loomed through the mist currently covering the capital, its stone facade a stoic sentinel amidst the chaos of wartime London. Eventually, the convoy pulled into the courtyard where a small crowd of officers and clerks had gathered. Brakes stepped out, wincing as his wounded arm caught on the doorframe. The medic at the farmhouse had cleaned and bandaged the graze from Smith's bullet, but the pain flared with every movement. Ford and Marks flanked him, their own injuries evident in their stiff postures.

Inside, the air was thick with the scent of ink, cigarette smoke, and over-brewed tea. The Chief Superintendent, Sir Harold Grayson, awaited them in his office, a cavernous room lined with maps and case files, the walls bearing the weight of a hundred investigations. When he stood to attention, they could see that he was a bear of a man whose stern face broke into a smile when Brakes entered the room.

"Brakes, you bloody marvel," he said, his voice like gravel as he extended a hand, then paused as he noted the sling cradling Brakes' arm. "Hell of a night, I hear."

Brakes managed a tired nod, sinking into a chair as Ford and Marks stood at ease behind him. "Hall is in custody, sir. Two shots—one to the shoulder, one to the leg. He'll live to face trial."

Grayson returned to his seat and leaned back, his chair creaking. "You've done what half the Yard thought impossible. The Parachute Murders, the Sock Murders—whatever the papers call them—solved in a single night. And you brought him in alive, no less." He gestured to a stack of telegrams on his desk. "Home Office is singing your praises. The RAF's calling it a miracle you survived that Spitfire."

"To be fair, sir, it is by the grace of the talents of the RAF that we stand before you." Brakes replied, but a moment later his jaw tightened. "Lost a good plane, though, and two constables are in hospital."

Grayson's expression sobered. "Aye, but they'll pull through. You kept the body count low, Brakes, and against a man who turned the skies into a slaughterhouse, no less. That's no small feat." Taking a decanter that sat on the desk, Grayson poured a measure of whisky and slid the glass across over to Brakes. "Drink. You've earned it."

Brakes hesitated before lifting the glass to his mouth and taking a sip, the amber liquid burning a path down his throat. The warmth dulled the ache in his arm, if not the unease in his gut. "Hall said something, sir," he said, setting the glass down. "Before we cuffed him. Hinted at something bigger. Accomplices, maybe."

Grayson's eyes narrowed, but he waved a dismissive hand. "The ravings of a cornered rat. We'll sweat him in interrogation, see what he's hiding. For now, you focus on healing. Doctor's waiting downstairs to patch you up properly."

Brakes nodded and slowly, he stood from his chair and left the office with Ford and Marks in tow. They eventually branched off once Brakes arrived at the medical room, which was a stark contrast to the battlefield of Suffolk thanks to its sterile space of antiseptic and starched linens. A doctor examined Brakes' arm, cleaning the wound with a grimace.

"Bullet grazed the muscle, nothing vital," he muttered, stitching with deft hands. "You'll need the sling for a week, maybe two. And no heroics, Inspector. Rest."

Brakes snorted, the idea of rest as foreign as peace in 1943. The doctor finished, securing the sling with a stern warning, and Brakes returned to the squad room where his team awaited. Marks was nursing a cup of tea, her knuckles bruised from the scuffle, while Ford polished his Enfield. The RAF pilot, Hawkins, had joined them, his flight jacket scuffed but his grin intact.

"Heard you're the hero of the hour, Inspector," Hawkins said, clapping Brakes on his good shoulder.

"Not me," Brakes replied, his voice low. "All of us. You kept that Lysander in the air longer than physics allowed."

Hawkins chuckled, but his eyes held the same haunted glint as the others. They'd faced near-death together, and the bond forged in that Suffolk field was unbreakable.

As the morning stretched on, Grayson and a handful of clerks eventually joined Brakes and his team in the squad room. Taking their seats, Brakes wearily stood to update everyone on the night's events.

The debriefing continued well into the afternoon, a marathon of reports and statements. Brakes recounted every detail—the Spitfire's strafing runs, the farmhouse assault and Hall's desperate stand. The clerks scribbled furiously, and Grayson nodded in approval, promising commendations for the entire team. By the time they finished, dusk was already creeping over London, the city's blackout curtains drawn tight against the threat of Luftwaffe raids.

As everyone began filing out one by one, Brakes lingered in the squad room. The maps on the walls, once marked with pins tracing Hall's murders, now felt like relics of a battle won, but Hall's final words still lingered.

"You're brooding, sir," Ford said, appearing at his side and offering Brakes a lopsided grin. "We got him; it's now up to the interrogators to worry about his nonsense."

Brakes managed a faint smile. "You're right, Ford. But I'll sleep better when we know he's alone in this."

The next morning, Brakes gathered his team in the courtyard, the air crisp with the promise of autumn. His arm, now properly treated, rested in a clean sling, the pain dulled by a night's fitful sleep. Ford, Marks, Parry, Shaw and Hawkins and a handful of constables who'd joined the Suffolk raid stood in a loose semicircle, their faces a mix of pride and fatigue.

"You lot," Brakes began, his voice steady as he looked around his team and those that had aided him in the capture of Fred Hall. "You're the finest I've ever worked with. We brought down a monster, and I'll never forget it."

"Just doing our job, sir," Ford muttered, unable to meet Brakes' gaze as he looked down at his feet. Marks simply nodded, the corners of her mouth tugging upwards into a smile.

"Wouldn't have trusted anyone else to have my back," she said proudly as Hawkins, who had taken to leaning against a lamppost, saluted Brakes lazily.

"Next time, Inspector, get me a plane with guns." Hawkins grinned, earning a ripple of laughter from the group as Brakes rolled his eyes, barely able to contain his own smile.

Stepping forward, Brakes began shaking hands with the team that had aided him in finally taking down the Parachute Murderer. A few clapped their hands to his good shoulder as he took a moment to exchange quiet words with each person present. They had been his lifeline in the chaos of war, an anchor in a raging sea. Now, with the case closed, it felt as if he was adrift.

He watched as the team began to disperse, their promises to meet for a pint once the dust settled lingering between them. When the last person finally left, Brakes took a moment to savour Scotland Yard one last time.

The building loomed before him, imposing as ever and now a memory of his time on the Parachute Murder case. He'd left instructions for the interrogators to press Hall hard, but answers would take time—time he didn't have today. Reaching a hand up to his head, Brakes tipped his hat to the building before finally turning to leave.

The train to Norwich waited at Liverpool Street Station, its steam engine hissing like a restless beast. Brakes boarded, his suitcase light but his thoughts heavy. The carriage was half-empty, filled with weary soldiers and civilians clutching ration books. He sank into a seat by the window, watching London's bombed-out skyline fade into the green blur of the countryside while the rhythm of the tracks lulled him.

Norwich station emerged from the haze of late morning, its platform bustling with families and servicemen. Brakes stepped off and scanned the crowd. There, by the ticket office stood Vera, her sharp eyes immediately softening when they landed on him before narrowing at the sight of the sling.

"Brakes, you daft man," she said as she strode forward, her voice a mix of exasperation and warmth. "Shot again, were you? We hear you had a run in with a madman in a plane?"

"Something like that, Vera. Got him, though." Brakes chuckled, wincing as she pulled him into a gentle hug, mindful of his arm. "I hear congratulations are in order for you too, Vera; you solved your very first case, and in the shadow of the Chief, no less. Well done you."

Vera pursed her lips, but her eyes gleamed with pride. "You always do. Now, come on; let's get you home before you find another lunatic to chase."

She led him to the waiting police car, its engine coughing to life as they trundled toward his cottage on the outskirts of Norwich. Vera's usual energy surfaced in full force, her chatter a comforting litany of scolds and concern. "You're only skin and bones, Brakes. When's the last time you ate a proper meal? And that arm—don't you dare lift a finger until it's healed. I've got stew on the stove for you, and you'll eat every bite."

Brakes let her words wash over him, the familiarity soothing the jagged edges of his nerves. The cottage came into view, its thatched roof and ivy-covered walls a haven amidst the war's turmoil. Once he was inside, the air smelled of woodsmoke and Vera's cooking, a stark contrast to the cordite and blood of the farmhouse. She bustled about, setting a bowl of stew before him, her hands lingering as if to reassure herself he was truly there.

As he ate, Brakes' mind drifted back to Hall. The interrogations would begin soon, peeling back the layers of his cryptic warning. Was there a network of killers, hidden in the war's chaos? Or was Hall playing one last game?

"You're miles away, Brakes," Vera said, her voice softening as she noted his distraction. "You've done your part. Let the Yard handle the rest."

He nodded, forcing a smile. "You're right, Vera. Just... tying up loose ends."

She snorted, clearing the table. "Loose ends'll be the death of you. Get some rest; that's an order."

Without protest, Brakes retreated to his armchair by the fire, the crackle of the burning logs a quiet counterpoint to the storm in his mind. The war raged on, its shadows long and unforgiving, but for now, he was home. Hall was behind bars, Brakes' team was safe, and Vera's stew had warmed his bones.

Yet as he closed his eyes, the echo of Hall's words lingered, a whisper of battles yet to come. For tonight, though, Brakes let the fire's glow hold the darkness at bay, his cottage a fragile sanctuary in a world at war.

Please enjoy a taster of Book Three, *Faith Brakes*.

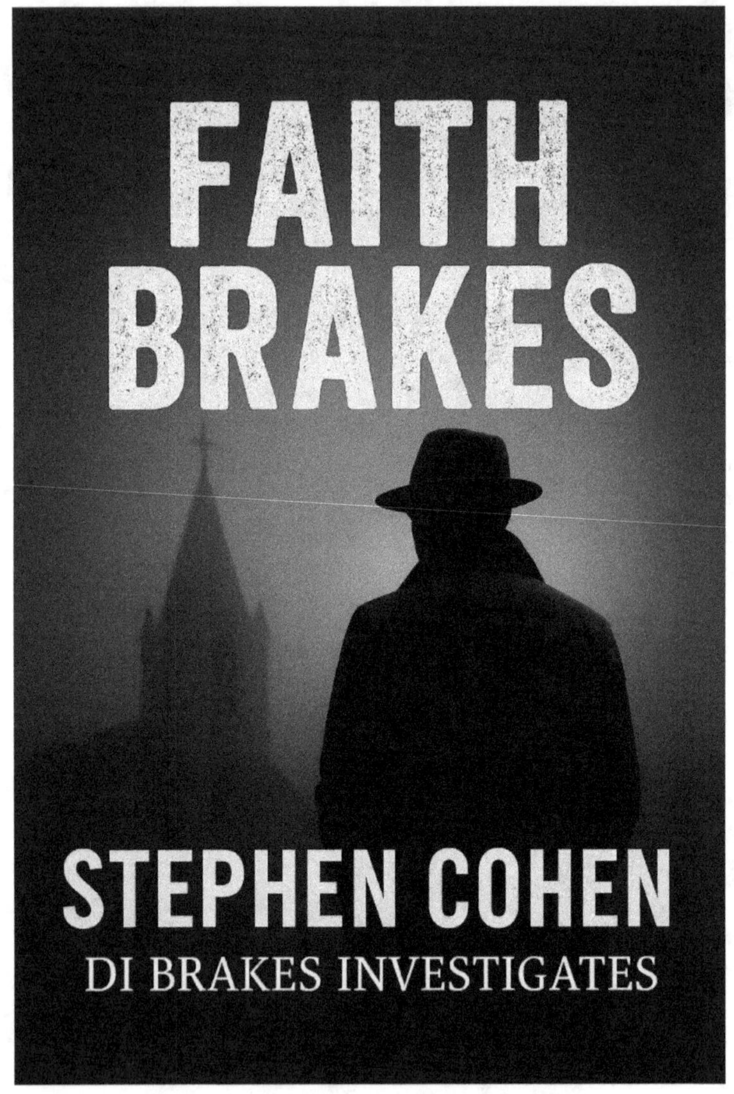

CHAPTER ONE

"Bring the car round, Vera; I think it's time we went home."

It had been a long, quiet day at the station and quite frankly, Detective Inspector Brakes had had enough. Instructing Vera to bring the car round, it didn't take long before they were driving away, the rain-slicked streets of Norwich gleaming under the sodium glow of the streetlights.

As they pulled up outside of Brakes' modest cottage that sat just on the outskirts of Norwich, he noticed the front door had been left open slightly. Stepping out of the car, Brakes tiredly wondered if his father had left it open for his arrival.

Right now, Brakes' parents were not getting along quite so well, so it had been decided that his father, Thomas, would stay with him. It had already been a few days since his dad's arrival from London and while it was strange to have someone else in his home, Brakes was glad to have the company.

He'd been looking forward to having a pint with his father all day; the old man had promised to regale a few more stories from his days as a beat copper, tales that Brakes was sure he would never tire of hearing.

Bidding Vera a good evening, Brakes watched as she headed home herself before turning back to his cottage. The chill autumn air was biting through his overcoat, and as he started towards the house, a prickle of unease crawled up his spine. It was unlike his father leave the door open. Thomas was meticulous in his habits—doors locked, windows latched even in the summer, always. Stepping towards the cottage, Brakes cautiously approached the door.

"Dad?" he called out, pushing the door wide open. The hallway was dark, the air heavy with a metallic tang that made his stomach lurch.

He flicked on the light and his world tilted.

Thomas Brakes lay sprawled across the living room floor, a neat hole in his temple. Blood pooled beneath his head, soaking into the rug. His eyes, wide and unseeing, stared at the ceiling. A glass of whiskey sat untouched on the side table, a silent witness to the violence.

"No," Brakes whispered, his knees buckling. He stumbled forward, fingers trembling as he checked for a pulse that he knew he wouldn't find. "No, no, no!" The word became a roar, raw and guttural, tearing from his chest. His father—his anchor, his hero—was gone.

A sharp rap at the door jolted him. He spun, hand instinctively reaching for his service pistol, which he wasn't carrying. Mrs. Hargreaves, his elderly neighbour, stood in the doorway, her face pale, eyes wide with fear. "Brakes, I heard a bang—I saw them!"

"Saw who?" his voice was a low growl, barely human.

"Two men. They came out of your house not ten minutes ago. One was tall, lanky, with a shaved head and a scar across his cheek. The other was shorter, stocky, with a red cap. You know, the type that the French wear, and he walked with a limp." The old woman gasped, her words coming out in a panicked rush. "They got into a black van—old, rusty, with a cracked windscreen. They sped off toward the river, down St. Ann's Lane."

Brakes mind snapped into focus, the details searing into his memory. "You're sure?"

She nodded, wringing her hands. "I'm so sorry, love. I called the police, but you got here first."

He didn't wait to hear more. Brakes was already next to his phone and dialling maniacally. The phone had barely rung once before it was picked up.

"Doug, it's me. Get to my place. Now."

Twenty minutes later, Brakes' neighbour had already left by the time his friend Doug Harper pulled up in his sleek blue coloured MG sports car. He was still in his RAF flight instructor's uniform, his broad frame filling the doorway as his familiar easy grin vanished the moment he saw Brakes, now crouched beside his father's body.

"Christ, Brakes," Doug breathed, kneeling beside him. "What happened?"

"They shot him," Brakes said, his voice flat. "Two men. I know what they look like, what they're driving. They're in Norwich, and I'm going to find them."

Brakes watched as Doug's jaw tightened. He had known Brakes' father from when they were lads, sneaking beers in the back garden while his old man pretended not to notice. To say Doug must have considered his father family would not surprise Brakes at all.

"Then we find them," Doug said, his words low and dangerous as he stood. "You and me. Let's go."

Brakes grabbed his coat, ignoring the arriving constables and the wail of sirens. Protocol could wait; Justice couldn't.

They took Doug's car, the MG engine roaring as they tore toward St. Ann's Lane. Brakes relayed Mrs. Hargreaves' description, his words clipped, precise. "Tall, scarred, shaved head. Short, limping, red cap. Black van, rusty, cracked windscreen. They're ours."

Doug nodded, his hands steady on the wheel as he scanned the streets. Brakes took in a ragged breath, his own gaze sweeping the streets that passed them by.

"We'll check every street, every pub, every bloody alley if we have to. They can't have gone far." Brakes growled. He was used to high-stakes missions, but this was personal.

Norwich's narrow lanes twisted around them, a labyrinth of brick and cobblestone. They started methodically, Doug driving, Brakes leaning out the window, scrutinising every vehicle, every face. The river district was first—warehouses, dive bars, places where men like the ones described might hide. Nothing. No black van, no scarred man, no red cap.

"Turn left," Brakes snapped as they reached a junction. His fingers drummed on the dashboard, his pulse a relentless hammer in his skull. "They're here, Doug. I can feel it."

They cruised past the Rose and Crown, its windows fogged with condensation. Brakes' eyes locked on a group of men that had congregated outside, but none of them matched the description Mrs. Hargreaves had given him.

"Keep going," he growled, his voice growing tighter, sharper.

They continued to methodically search pub after pub, street after street. The night deepened, and the city seemed to mock them with each turn. A black van turned out to be a delivery truck. A man in a red cap was just a teenager, not a limping killer. Each dead end stoked the fire in Brakes' chest, his grief hardening into something darker, more primal.

"Slow down," he barked as they passed the Dog's Head, a grimy pub on the edge of the industrial estate. A flicker of movement caught his eye—a man stepping out, tall, his shaved head glinting under the streetlight. Brakes' heart surged, but the man turned, revealing an unscarred face.

"Damn it!" He slammed his fist into the dashboard, the pain barely registering.

"Easy, mate," Doug said, his voice calm but firm. "We'll find them. Stay sharp."

"Sharp?" Brakes' laugh was bitter, jagged. "They killed him, Doug. My dad. Shot him like he was nothing. I'm not stopping until they're in the ground."

They pressed on, the MG weaving through Norwich's arteries. The Three Tuns, the Black Horse, the old warehouses by the docks—every stop was a fresh wound, every empty lead a twist of the knife. Brakes' frustration grew, a living thing clawing at his insides. He pictured his father's face, the blood, the silence, and his hands clenched until his knuckles whitened.

At the Anchor, a dockside pub reeking of stale beer and desperation, Brakes stormed inside, ignoring Doug's call to wait. He scanned the room, his gaze similar to a sharpened blade, cutting through the crowd. A man in a corner booth wore a red cap, but he was thin, no menace. Brakes' vision blurred with rage. He grabbed the man's shoulder, spinning him around. "Where's your mate?" he snarled.

The man blinked, confused. "What? I don't—"

"Brakes!" Doug was there, pulling him back, his grip like iron. "He's not one of them. Come on."

Brakes shook him off, chest heaving. "They're slipping away, Doug. Every second we waste, they're getting further."

"We'll get them," Doug said, steering him outside. "But you need to hold it together. For Thomas."

The mention of his father's name was a punch to the gut. Brakes sagged against the car, the fight draining out of him for a moment, replaced by a bone-deep ache. "He didn't deserve this," he whispered. "He was just... here. Visiting me."

"I know," Doug said quietly. "And we'll make it right. Together."

They climbed back into the MG, the engine's growl a faint echo of Brakes' fury. The city sprawled before them, endless, unyielding. Somewhere in its shadows, two men hid, their hands stained with Thomas Brakes' blood. Brakes' eyes burned, his resolve a blade honed to a lethal edge. He would find them. And when he did, there would be no mercy.

The Old Barge Inn on King Street hummed with the low murmur of Friday night regulars, the air thick with the scent of ale and damp wood. Inspector Brakes pushed through the heavy oak door, his eyes scanning the dimly lit room while Doug stood beside him, a solid presence at his shoulder. The weight of the hunt pressed on Brakes' chest, every nerve taut, every shadow a potential lead. They'd been at it for hours, scouring Norwich's underbelly, and the Old Barge was their last stop before exhaustion forced a pause.

Brakes' gaze swept the bar, locking onto two men at a corner table. One was tall, lanky, a jagged scar slicing across his cheek, his shaved head gleaming under the flickering light. The other, shorter, stocky, wore a red cap tilted low, his left leg stiff as he shifted in his seat. Brakes' blood turned to ice, then fire.

It was them.

The scarred man's eyes met Brakes and widened in shock, as if he'd seen a ghost. The red-capped man froze, his pint halfway to his lips. For a split second, the world held its breath. Then the scarred man bolted, shoving the table aside, glasses crashing to the floor. His partner scrambled after him, limping but fast, the crowd parting in confusion.

"Move!" Brakes roared, sprinting after them, Doug right behind him. The men barrelled through the back door into Old Barge Yard, a narrow, cobbled alley slick with rain. Brakes' boots pounded the stones, his heart a war drum. The men were quick, desperation lending them speed, but Brakes was fuelled by something darker—rage, grief, vengeance.

The yard opened to the river's edge where a sleek motor launch bobbed against the quay, its engine already rumbling. The scarred man leapt aboard, the red-capped man stumbling after, nearly slipping into the black water. The boat's engine roared and it surged forward, cutting a white wave through the Wensum.

Brakes skidded to a halt at the water's edge, his eyes locking onto a smaller craft moored nearby—a battered single-engine skiff, barely more than a dinghy.

"Doug, get the car!" he shouted, already leaping into the skiff. "Follow them by road!"

Doug hesitated for a fraction of a second, then nodded, sprinting back toward the MG parked outside the pub. Brakes yanked the skiff's starter cord, the engine coughing to life with a reluctant sputter. He gunned it, the little craft lurching forward, its bow slapping the water as he gave chase.

The motor launch was a beast, sleek and powerful, slicing south toward the broads' sprawling waterways. Brakes' skiff, underpowered and sluggish, strained against the current, its engine whining in protest. He leaned forward, as if willpower alone could close the gap, his knuckles white on the tiller. "Come on, you bastard," he growled, urging the engine. "Give me more."

The launch's wake rocked the skiff, water splashing over the sides, soaking Brakes' coat. He could still see them—the scarred man at the helm, the red-capped man glancing back, his face a mask of panic. They were heading for the open waterways, where the broads' maze of channels and reeds could swallow them whole. Brakes' jaw clenched. He wouldn't let them vanish. Not after what they'd done.

The city's lights faded behind him, the river widening as it fed into the broader network of the Norfolk Broads. The launch's speed was relentless, its silhouette shrinking against the dark horizon. Brakes pushed the skiff harder, the engine's scream drowning out the slap of waves, but the gap widened. His heart pounded, frustration clawing at him.

"No!" he shouted, the word lost to the wind. The launch rounded a bend, and just like that, it was gone, swallowed by the night.

Brakes slammed his fist against the skiff's side, the sharp jolt of pain a fleeting distraction from the fury boiling inside. He eased off the throttle, the engine's whine dropping to a defeated sputter. The broads stretched out around him, silent and vast, offering no answers. He'd lost them.

With a curse, he turned the skiff back toward the Old Barge, the journey slower now, the fire in his chest smouldering but unextinguished. He tied up at the quay and stormed back into the pub, his coat dripping, his eyes blazing. The patrons fell silent, sensing the storm in his stride.

"Who were they?" Brakes demanded, his voice cutting through the hush. He moved from table to table, leaning in close, his presence a blade. "Two men, one scarred, one limping with a red cap. They were here. You saw them. Talk."

Most shrank back, mumbling denials, but an old man at the bar, his hands trembling around a pint, met Brakes' gaze.

"I know one of 'em," he said, voice low. "The tall one, with the scar. Name's Victor Crane. Shady sort, always in trouble. Don't know where he lives, mind."

"Victor Crane," Brakes repeated, the name searing into his memory. It was something—more than he'd had an hour ago. "And the other?"

The old man shook his head. "Never seen him before."

Brakes pressed the rest of the room, but no one else spoke up. Either they didn't know, or they were too scared to say. He left the pub, the weight of the name Victor Crane his only tether to the men who'd killed his father.

Heading toward the town centre, he was halfway down King Street when Doug's MG screeched to a stop beside him. Doug leaned out, his face grim.

"I followed them as far as I could, Brakes. Kept to the roads parallel to the river, but once they hit the broads, I lost sight. Too many channels, too dark."

Brakes nodded, his jaw tight. "I got a name. Victor Crane. The tall one."

Doug's eyes narrowed. "It's a start. We'll find him."

Brakes climbed into the car, the night pressing in around them. The man had slipped through his fingers, but the hunt was far from over. Victor Crane was out there, and Brakes would tear the broads apart to find him. For his father. For justice. For blood.

Doug drove Brakes home in silence and upon arrival they were met with what seemed like every officer on the Norwich force, and to Brakes' surprise, even the Chief was in attendance.

"Brakes! Over here!" yelled the Chief.

"Wait by the car," Brakes instructed Doug tiredly and immediately started making his way over to the Chief, who greeted him with a serious yet mournful look in his eyes.

"Sorry for your loss, Inspector." the Chief murmured. Brakes simply nodded, doing his best to plaster a sober expression to his face and hoping no emotion peeked through. The Chief quickly sell silent and stood rooted to the spot, staring at Brakes and searching for a crack in his façade. Then, clearing his throat, Brakes' superior continued.

"You realise of course that, under normal circumstances, you wouldn't be allowed anywhere near this case," he explained carefully, still watching Brakes closely. Brakes simply nodded stiffly in response. "But, in light of the fact we are at war and deeply under-manned, you will have to be a part of it."

A surge of relief flooded through Brakes. Relief that he would see his father's murderers brought to justice, relief that he would be able to see the light of hope fade from their eyes.

"Thank you, Chief," he said tightly, hoping his anger and grief would not betray his voice. "Yes, this case is personal, and yes, I am truly bereaved. But I will try my best not to let you down."

The Chief nodded, his posture rigid as he said his next words. "Well, you can't stay here, Brakes. Do you have anywhere else you can stay for a couple of nights while we clear the scene?" he asked.

"I can stay with my friend Doug at the base, sir," Brakes replied stiffly and without another word, he walked past the Chief and headed into his cottage to collect a few of his belongings.

When he entered the house, he stopped for a moment to gaze into his living room. His father's body had already been taken to the morgue, but the bloodstained rug was still there, the patch of blood darker than Brakes remembered.

As he turned away from the scene, the memory of his father's corpse lingered, now imprinted on his mind.

229

DI Brakes Investigates – Book 4 in this WWII crime fiction series is coming soon. Use the following link to sign up for my newsletter, release dates, un-released facts and more:-

https://books2read.com/author/stephen-cohen/subscribe/1/207713/

You can also find me on Linktree, social media links. Subscribe and follow me:-

https://linktr.ee/stephencohen

A personal note from the author:

Thank you for reading book 2 in my new crime series. Please don't forget to leave a review, follow and subscribe to my channels and newsletter to keep up to date with upcoming new releases.

Thank you for your support.